LAVISH LOVE

A BLAZIN' LOVE NOVELLA

JA'NESE DIXON

PUBLISHING

ALSO BY JA'NESE DIXON

THE BLAZIN' LOVE SERIES

Blazin' Love (Contemporary Romance)

Platinum Love (Book 1)

Privileged Love (Book 2)

Exclusive Love (Book 3)

Chosen Love (Book 4)

Special Love (Book 5)

Absolute Love (Book 6)

Pretend for Me (A Short Story)

Devoted Love (Book 7)

Select Love (Book 8)

Lavish Love (Book 9)

Total Love (Coming January 2019)

Steamy Sensations Holiday Love

ISBN-13: 978-1-950405-12-1 (paperback)

Printed in the United States of America.

TABLE OF CONTENTS

SNEAK PEEK: ROCKSTAR SECRETS

ABOUT LAVISH LOVE

Ho... Ho... Ho...

It's Christmas.

The little Santa in the hotel lobby is shady AF as I do the walk of shame. I accepted this assignment with one caveat: Don't land in Mateo's bed.

I'm Alexandria Martinez. I'm a globetrotter specializing in international trade. After almost ten years in business, Platinum Prestige is considering global expansion. And I'm questioning if I'm the woman for the job.

Mateo is dangerous for my heart yet beneficial for the next phase of our growth. He agrees to mentor me for the next six months in exchange for pretending to be his doting fiancé over the holidays.

I agree, and the Latin don Juan slips a rock the size of Texas on my finger, and the weight of it and his life force me to define love, happiness, and the true meaning of Christmas.

I expect snow and lights. I expect him to flirt and lavish me with the best his wealth provides. But what I didn't expect was romance and passion and my willingness to let him in again.

Should I trust the lessons bore from heartbreak? Or should I embrace the love budding amidst the concrete around my heart?

Mateo seems to think the answer lies in the gift of Christmas. And now I'm starting to believe maybe he's right.

CHAPTER 1

"*H*ello, handsome…" I whisper, brushing a hand across the cold coated paper. The slight shake of the magazine makes it hard to focus on the bold headline—Latino Businessperson of the Year. His thick black wavy hair flows away from his face, his bedroom eyes whisper, *Remember me.* And I do.

The sound of laughter invades my private moment with Mateo Rodriquez. My eyes dart to my open office door and back to the man who has invaded my dreams ever since he called Platinum Prestige a week ago.

According to Hunter, one of my best friends and business partners, Mateo contacted us about importing supplies and asked for me by name. I haven't returned his call because quite frankly I'm scared. Then I went to the corner store for a Coke and there he was on the magazine rack.

I've unintentionally kept up with his career. Here

and there. Not going out of my way, not avoiding it. It's hard to ignore him when the man is featured in magazines and on television shows. And now he's on top of the list of the Most Powerful Latinos in Business.

The steady cadence of my breathing is an act I've perfected. I'm the big bad Alexandria Martinez. I don't take shit from anybody, and I live by my own rules. But with him, it was different. I was different.

My invincible, artificial superpowers seemed to have a loophole. Mateo had me ready to leave my parents, Texas, and my life behind until my grandfather and my mother forbade *any* involvement with him.

A sudden tremble spreads through my entire body. I wonder what they'd say about him now. The kid they ran off that is a billionaire on the cover of a national magazine. My heart twists, and I stare at Mateo. I've begged for him to give my heart back after fifteen years, but my stubborn soul still wants him. The man that embodies everything I shouldn't desire. But I do.

I have to get this longing in check before I call him.

"What's that?" Charlee slips Mateo from my line of sight. "Aye, Papi."

"Give it back." I swipe at the air with the desk between us. "You're supposed to be on maternity leave. Why are you not at home?"

"Because somebody asked to see Raine." She rolls her eyes in my direction. "Why does he look familiar?"

"Uh...it's a new issue. I want to see the baby." I reach

for the magazine, and she dips out of my reach again. This is what happens when you work with your best friends. We're prone to reverting back to our non-professional behavior. I should have closed my door.

"I may forget names, but I know faces. Damn baby brain." Her head wags, and I chuckle. "I forgot the pin to our security system the other day. The operator called, and I'm so glad Darius was right behind me. Did you know they give a $250 ticket if a cop responds to a false alarm? Ask me how I know." She's thumbing through the pages talking to herself. "Mateo…Mateo…."

"He's just a guy on the cover of the magazine," I say, and the butterflies in my stomach call my bluff because Mateo was never just a guy.

"Charlee Raine…" Darius calls from down the hall. But her husband's call doesn't disrupt Charlee's struggle to summons the distant memories from college.

"You're going to make me miss the baby." I walk to the doorway and peak out around the corner.

When Ben had the floor remodeled, he made the focal point the sitting area. It's where we gather. Right now, they're crowded around Peyton, holding a bundle of pink minky.

"I want to hold her."

"I got it." Charlee shakes the magazine in my direction. "You used to tutor him. When was that?"

Oh hell. Why does her baby brain have to turn off

now? I chew on the inside of my lip, praying Charlee changes the subject.

"How are the boys enjoying their little sister?"

"Ethan loves it. Little D isn't impressed." She answers without looking in my direction. "Harper..." Charlee passes the magazine, and I want to disappear.

"Charlee, stop teasing Alex. Look at her face." Harper pulls me close, rubbing my back, then she looks down. "Oh, I saw him last week."

"You did?" I face Harper.

"Yeah, he remembered me from school and asked about you. He's trying to get his family here for the holidays or something like that. I didn't catch all of the details."

"So, you gave him our number?" I ask. This is all starting to make sense. Harper and her husband Liam own Walsh Executive Jets.

"Yes, was I not supposed to?" She lifts an inquisitive eyebrow.

"Of course, we're expanding our business, and he may need our services," I mutter, relieved when she places the magazine in my hand until Charlee retakes it.

"That was last week. Refresh my memory. We knew him in undergrad?"

"Let me see." Hunter walks over.

"I was his English tutor. Damn." I snatch the magazine back.

"Touchy…touchy." Charlee folds her arms with a tilt to her head.

"I'm not touchy. It's nothing. Now, let me hold the baby." I face Harper, who's now cradling Raine in her arms.

"Not until you wash your hands," Charlee says.

"Leave it alone, Charlee Raine." Darius places a hand on her shoulder. "Wash your hands. You're next."

I take his out.

I walk past the offices toward the break room. This is the executive floor of Platinum Prestige, an elite concierge service. We—Hunter, Harper, Charlee, Parker, Chase, Taylor, Payton, Ryann, Jordan, and I—started almost nine years ago. Ten women with guy names who have built and maintain a solid sisterhood and a lucrative business. We've dubbed ourselves the GIB—guys in black —because when you have ten *bad-ass* women strolling into a meeting dressed in all black, we're a sight to behold.

I stop at the sink turning on the hot water. It trickles over my fingertips, as I rerun the conversation in my head. I didn't mean to snap at Charlee. I owe her an apology.

I return to the sitting area, and Raine is still the center of their attention. I loop my arm through Charlee's and rest my head on her shoulder.

"Sorry," we whisper in unison, laughing it off.

"You know I don't mean any harm, Alex."

"I overreacted." I glance up into Charlee's eyes.

"Why?" Harper asks.

"I don't know. We have unfinished business, I guess." He's the one I let get away because I didn't have the courage to stand up to my family. It's an old regret that cuts deep.

My guys, graciously, let my little attitude go. I cradle Raine in my arms. She has a button nose, rosy cheeks, and jet-black curls like her mother, but her wise eyes resemble her father's. I inhale her fresh baby scent.

"Darius, are you planning for one more?" I tease.

"No, I want my body back. But I agreed to table the talk until Raine is two." Charlee answers, glancing up into his eyes as he wraps an arm around her waist. The way she leans into his body holds a sense of security and peace. She's a riot, and most men tried to tame her. But not Darius, he laughs at her quick wit, bad singing, and protects her fragile heart.

Darius loves Charlee.

How does it feel to be wholly accepted and loved?

Charlee and her family leave a while later. We stand around counting all the babies born into our family with Raine, Hunter's baby girl, Drew, and Ryann's baby boy Xavier. After a half-hour of chatting, the guys head back to their offices.

"Alex, can you stop by my office?" Hunter asks.

"Sure." I follow her down the hall with the magazine gathered to my chest. We sit at the same time as she extends her hand. I glance at Mateo and reluctantly let him go.

"I can't believe the name didn't ring a bell." She flips the pages, and mid-turn, her eyes met mine.

She returns the seven dollar instigator. I should have waited until I got home to read it but his eyes...they kept calling me. It's one thing to hear about his success, seeing him again awakens old feelings and old mistakes.

Hunter reclines in her chair. I've known her since elementary school, but the woman in front of me has transformed before our eyes.

"Is this cool with you? Reaching out to him and the possibility of working with him?"

I shrug. Not my most eloquent response, but it's all I got.

"I'm in an unusual predicament. I want to consider our options as a brand and leverage our growing popularity. However, we are nine guys down between pregnancies, newborns, or new marriages. I need to lean on you at least until I deliver this baby. And with Zoe turning thirteen, I can't oversee this." She rubs her belly in slow circular motions. "You're the most efficient, dependable, and organized of our bunch, which is saying a lot. You'll have our full support, but you have to be our anchor. Can I count on you?"

"Yes." I sit up.

"Even if it means working with Mateo?"

I shift in the chair under her intense gaze. She

knows secrets about my life that I haven't shared with all of the guys. It wasn't until Ryann told us about her father murdering her mother that I finally gave myself permission to think about my mother and my biological father as my parents.

Hunter knows how somedays it's hard to live in my skin. Mateo thriving in his Latino, Dominican skin makes it difficult to stew in my hidden insecurities.

I'm a grown-ass woman still afraid to stand up to my mother and accept half of my genetic makeup. I'm a coward.

"Yeah, sure. That was years ago. What do you have in mind?"

Her long pause makes me uncomfortable. Is she second-guessing her decision?

"For the record, I'm respecting your privacy, but you're safe here. We're not pressed to make this happen. Understand?"

"Yes. Tell me what you have in mind."

She nods, reaching in her side drawer. "I think having an idea of what to expect if we enter the international market. Legislation, tax considerations, expenses, viable services to provide. I guess we need to know the feasibility. And whether it's something we truly want to explore."

I nod. All of the partners work with Platinum Prestige, but only Hunter, her husband Ben, and I work here full time.

"According to this article, Mateo would be the

perfect person to help us get a clear picture. We could also talk with Liam since he has an extension of their business overseas. Darius too." I offer for her consideration. The guys have married astute and successful businessmen.

"That's right. You'll be our liaison, and I'll differ to your judgment."

"What type of deadline are we looking at?" This is the most significant assignment I've been given.

"We don't have to decide, but having enough information to sit the guys down by the end of the year would be cool."

"So, by our holiday girl's trip?" That's less than a month away.

"Oh yeah, that would be a perfect time. No kids. No husbands." She smiles at the thought, and so do I. The plan is to spend a weekend in Las Vegas.

"Jo, you about ready? Because I know you're hungry." Ben stops just inside the office. "Hey, Alex." He waves.

Hunter's eyes shift, and her love for him washes over the room. The dynamics of our relationships have changed. All but two of us are married. I'm the only one with neither a husband or a child.

Watching each guy find love and marry it equally joyous and isolating. I'm gaining brothers and precious godchildren, but a part of me is losing my sisters. Our tight circle is no longer a circle of ten, and I tell myself I'm happy about it.

"Hey. Where are y'all going to eat?" I stand.

"I hope home. This baby is a picky eater." Hunter starts gathering her stuff.

"Zoe started your favorite, spaghetti." Ben picks up her bag, tossing it over his shoulder.

"Cooking, about to turn thirteen…" I rub my hands over my arms covered in goosebumps. Zoe is Ben's niece that he and Hunter raise. "Next thing she'll be heading off to college."

"Don't go there. Someone becomes a puddle of tears." Ben smiles with his eyes glued on Hunter.

"I can't help it. Watch when you have kids. One minute they're babies the next they're leaving. God, I hate crying." She fans her eyes. "Please change the subject."

"I'll call Mateo when I get to my office."

Hunter nods. "Ben, Alex's going to research the global expansion."

"Great. Let me know if you need a hand." He adds.

"I'll have this handled in no time."

"I have no doubts. But if it becomes too much, promise you'll walk away." Her eyes are stern.

"Yes, Mother Hunter."

"I'm serious. You were a different person with him."

"What do you mean?"

Mateo and I kept our relationship between the four walls of my apartment. He met the guys and spent time with them, but I never went into detail. We all were dating and adjusting to life outside the sphere of our parents.

"Let's go, Jo. Zoe will fuss like her Mamma Jo if the food gets cold."

Hunter wags her head walking into the hallway. "Who wants to spend time slaving over a stove to serve cold food?"

"Hunt, what did you mean?" I place a hand on her arm.

"Give us a second."

"I'll give you five. I need to get something from my office." He kisses her cheek, and Hunter waits for him to enter his office.

"Alex, you laughed more, you let your hair down, you stopped caring about your mother's wants and wishes. You stopped hiding. You were different." She gathers my hands in hers. "I knew the moment you two broke it off. The moment he boarded that plane to New York, he took a piece of you with him."

"Why are you telling me this now?"

"Part of me wonders if we should have asked more questions. You've never been open about your relationships, but when he left, you changed." Her lips are tense around the words. "I want you happy, Alex. Truly happy. Not trapped in the life of your mother's making."

"My mother has nothing to do with it."

"Lying doesn't change the truth." Her quick retort surprises me.

I step closer, forcing myself to remain calm. I avoid conversations about my parents for a reason. "I know you mean well, but..."

"Call it mother's intuition, advice from a person who loves you, or a gentle nudge from your boss. What if you walked into the new year embracing the amazing woman you are? *All* of you."

"Ready?"

We face Ben over her shoulder. Emotions swirl into a sinking knot in my stomach. My unsettling thoughts concerning Mateo. The bomb dropped by Hunter. The phone call I agreed to make knowing the moment I hear his voice I'll remember all the reasons I love him and all the reasons I can't have him.

"Have a good night?" I force a fake smile on my face and a chipper tone in my voice. "I'll see you guys Monday."

"Alex...Alex..."

I walk off, closing my office door, unable to breathe deep enough to chase away the sting of her words. *All of me*. What does that mean?

Hunter doesn't understand. No one does. The duality inside me, one championed as Black Girl Magic and hashtagged as melanin. But the other always made to reflect a sense of wrongness and shunned by my parents and grandfather.

I drop in my chair and flip the magazine face down.

I deliberately take long draws of air in and out of

my nose until my heartbeat is normal. The phone stares at me.

"Mateo's an old friend," I whisper, dropping my head back, brushing my tongue over my dry lips. I know it's not true, but I'm embracing this "old friend" disillusionment like a life jacket because this call isn't for me but my team.

I tuck my personal feelings into a tiny box in the dark corner of my mind and dial the number I still know by heart. The sooner I call him, the sooner I'll get it over with, and I can return to my life without Mateo Rodriquez.

CHAPTER 2

"*M*ateo!"

I toss the damn magazine aside. Every step I make in my career puts my family in jeopardy. People read billionaire, and my parents and siblings become targets.

"Mamá. ¿Por qué estás haciendo esto difícil?" Asking my mother why she's making this difficult is like asking why the sun shines. *That's just the way it is.*

"Hijo estoy bien."

"It's not fine," I mumble through clenched teeth. This conversation is useless. I've tried to hire security guards, and I've threatened to move back home. Nothing works. She's stubborn as a mule.

"Tell me about your lady friend." She transitions to English, and for the first time since calling her, I smile.

"You're still working with your tutor?"

"Si…huh, yes."

"And I don't have a lady friend."

Her rapid Spanish flies through the line. I sit back, letting it rain over me. Her constant complaint about me being too focused on my career and how she'll never have grandchildren.

"You don't love me," she declares. I can hear the pucker of her lips.

"I love you more than anything and anyone in the world. But I'm too busy to date."

"Too busy for love? That's so American of you. You're never too busy for family. Careers don't love you back."

"Come here for Christmas. We can celebrate as a family under one roof. I'll take care of everything."

"How? You don't cook."

"Don't worry about the food. I'll send a private flight for everyone. Please, Mamá."

"I'm scared to fly."

"I'll fly there and fly back with you." Her grunt fills the line. I let her think about it, holding my breath.

"…tal vez."

Her hesitant maybe gives me hope. "Thank you."

"I didn't say yes."

"But you didn't say no. You are tougher than the most educated businessmen in the world."

Her laughter floats through the line, and my heart smiles. "You are the worst, always pushing to have your way."

"No existe gran talento sin gran voluntad." My

parents told me these words as I boarded a flight to Texas on a full scholarship. There is no great talent without great will. And my determination is indestructible, especially when faced with protecting the ones I love.

"You took our words and have exceeded our prayers. It brings peace to my soul." She has a sense of joy in her voice.

"Promise you'll consider it. I worry." I swallow back the plea nearing the tip of my tongue. I will get them here. Safe.

"I'll consider it. Now let me grab your father so you can tell us about this article."

My father jumps on the line, and we talk. Somehow, we go from the article to my press tour, to my mother telling me about her friends' grandchildren again despite us having the same conversation last week. My father heads back out to his garage, leaving us alone. And she questions my will, I'm clearly her son.

I shake my head at my spitfire mom who stands inches over four feet, a giant in my eyes. I could remind her that my brother and sister are handlings the kid quota without my assistance. However, this will only drag the talk into her overarching justification that I'm the oldest, and I should have a wife by now.

A wife, Gloria Rodriquez, refuses to acknowledge, which is my business. My mother claims the American culture has edged out the core of who I am and what I mean to this family as the eldest son. They sent me to

America to succeed, and I have, except my parents, always planned for me to return. So, instead of interjecting and swapping one sore spot for another, I sit back and respond where appropriate.

Susan, my assistant, steps inside my office. She mocks, bringing a receiver to her ear.

Who is it? I mouth.

Alexandria, on line two, she responds. I stare at the flashing white light.

"Mom, I have an important call to take. I'll call you tonight with the flight details."

"Your father and I will discuss it."

"Te amo, Mamá." We say our goodbyes, and I press two. "Alexandria."

I exhale, not recognizing my voice or the erratic cadence of my heart. The shift from concern about my parents to her on the line gives my spirit whiplash.

"Hey, …I…God…it feels good to hear your voice." Her soothing tone sounds different yet familiar.

"How long has it been?" I ask to hear her talk again, and I'm rewarded with her sultry laugh.

"I will not say because it will age us both."

"I'm sure you haven't aged a year. How are you?"

Alexandria exhales a shaky breath matching my own. "I'm good. It's the holiday season. Between business and shopping for my nieces and nephews, I have a full plate. What about you?"

The smile in her voice sends a fresh wave of awareness through my body. We were once something special, but timing and circumstances were against us. That was over fifteen years ago. In my pursuit of success, I forgot to turn around, thankfully fate hasn't dismissed the possibility of us.

"I'd rather tell you in person."

Her soft gasp pulls me forward in my chair. "You're here? In Austin?"

"No, I'll be there in the morning. How about brunch? You select the place and time, and I'll be there." I have no plans of flying to Austin, but all I need is her agreement to meet with me. I open my calendar, scanning my jam-packed day. "Say yes, Alexandria."

"Yes…but…this is a meeting between old friends, and I have business matters to discuss with you."

"Aye… Alexandria…building a wall already?" The man in me, aiming to win at everything I put my mind to, challenges her declaration.

"It's not a wall but boundaries, *Mateo Rodriquez*."

"Boundaries? What are those?" My accent is thick because I remember how it always brought a sly grin and an eye roll from her. The proper beauty and her doting immigrant.

"Which is exactly why we need to establish them before we see each other."

"Aye…*mi querida*."

"And none of that? Keep those sweet words to yourself."

"What?" I mock shock, and her laughter spills over.

"Don't tell me you've lost your sense of adventure and fun."

"I know how to have a good time like anyone else. But you Mateo have always been slicker than oil. I refuse to get caught up in your plans."

"That's how you see me?" My gruff question hangs between us. I don't expect her to respond to my bait. That would be too easy.

"Have you changed?" She counters.

"Hummmm…" I sit back, propping my feet up. The view of New York City from my desk is why I bought the building. The cars crawl through evening traffic, and a flickering Christmas tree in an office across the way captures my attention.

"Do you still talk with your mother several times a day? Eat two eggs, dry toast, with fresh strawberries every morning but Sunday. Run five miles, Monday through Friday." She rattles off a list as if she's peering at my life in a crystal ball. The more she talks, the more my chest tightens.

"Am I that predictable?" I type a quick message to Susan. *Reschedule all appointments over the weekend and arrange a flight to Austin tonight.*

"It's why you're so successful. Speaking of success, congratulations. You always said you wanted to live an unforgettable life. It seems you're living your dream."

"Success is a double-edged sword, and dreams are fleeting." I watch the snow falling. The ceiling to floor windows makes me feel less alone when my days and nights are long. I watch the sunrise and set. I marvel as the seasons change in vivid colors unique to New York.

I never complain. Because no matter how many days and nights I sit behind my computer relentless in my pursuit of expanding my business, it's better than the life of poverty I left behind in Santo Domingo. However, on the heels of my talk with my mother, and now Alexandria, I wonder if life is passing me by.

"Billionaire problems?"

"Aye, what about you? I saw Harper, and she told me about your business. You didn't join your family's company?"

"I did for a while after graduating. Then we started Platinum Prestige."

"Still clawing for your independence, *querida*?"

"No, I...I couldn't turn down the offer to work with my best friends. We'll celebrate our tenth anniversary time next year. Which is part of the reason for my call. I'd like to pick your brain about the advantages and disadvantages of entering the global market."

"You waited fifteen years to pick my brain?"

"Yes...no...well, maybe." She sighs. "You called, and I read the article in the magazine. It makes sense to consult with an authority before embarking on this type of business shift."

"Are you asking as a personal friend or a prospective client?"

"Both and neither. I'm asking between Alexandria and Mateo. Fill in the blanks."

Fill in the blanks. I can fill in the blanks with all types of ideas. Several I'm sure she'd object to over the phone.

The slight squeak of the door pulls my eyes in that direction. Susan enters with a yellow note. She drops it on my desk and slips out. The airplane is prepped for my departure. I lower my feet to the floor.

"Let's table the discussion until brunch. Tell me when and where."

"It's Saturday. I usually work from home. We can have brunch at my place if you still prefer home-cooked meals or there's Torsion. And Mateo, this is in the professional capacity."

She's offering to cook for me in the professional capacity. I keep the thought to myself. "Right… Professional brunch at your place. You'll cook, and I'll bring the beverages." We talk for a few minutes while I shut down my computer. We exchange cellphone numbers, and I promise to text her when I land. Once I drop my wallet in my pocket, I ask, "Do you require anything else *mi querida?*"

"No, just you."

My eyes blur with desire, and the familiar heat of anticipation burns through me. Those three words are etched in every passionate memory with her.

"I didn't mean to…you asked and… Maybe this isn't such a good idea."

"Is this more of your boundaries talk, Alexandria?"

The woman I remember was passionate in bed and out. I wonder if she still lurks behind these *boundaries*.

"No, I don't want to give you the wrong impression, and I'm seeing someone."

"Seeing someone?" I lower back into my chair. "What's his name? How long have you been seeing him?"

"Huh…"

"Would he approve of you cooking and sharing a private meal with another man? Someone you lived with. Someone you once loved."

"I…he…we—"

"If…you were my woman—"

"But, I'm not." Her voice cuts through our rapid exchange.

I can't contain my laughter. "Fine. He's invited to join us *if* this man exists. I'll speak to you when I land. Adiós."

I disconnect the call the moment I hear her tight goodbye. She's always lingered in the depths of my mind, but I never thought of her moving on, getting married, having children. My face drops to my hands.

What if I'm too late?

Too late for a second chance with Alexandria? Too late to protect my family from the scum trying to weasel money out of me.

Frustration swells inside me until it erupts in a wave. I let it flow until my lungs collapse flat near defeat.

I lift my head, and my gaze settles on a tiny snowflake taking a whimsical journey through the air, landing on the glass. In a few hours, the entire city will be covered, transformed from a concrete jungle to a winter wonderland. My life is like the snowflake, slow and steady until I accomplish my goals. All I need is a plan to transform this situation in my favor. That thought freezes in my brain.

What if Alexandria can help me get my parents here? I would need more than an airplane and a reason for them to come here for Christmas. A reason that will give me time to neutralize any threats in Santo Domingo.

Alexandria, ...and my parents.

What will bring them to the US without question? I drum my fingers on the desk.

"Weddings, babies, and funerals," I whisper, trying to corral my options.

"You'll figure it out. But for now, the car is waiting downstairs." Surprised, my head jerks to the doorway, and Susan's in the hallway buttoning up her black heavy winter coat. The sparkle of a diamond stops me.

"Congratulations." I walk over, turning off the light.

She wiggles her hand, making the ring dance under the lights. "I planned to tell you. Apparently, my constant snooping ruined Jerrick's surprise."

"See, you thought he was cheating." I chuckle. We walk through the office, the last ones leaving for the weekend.

"I was wrong. He was planning a surprise engagement party. Wait…you knew, didn't you?"

"I bet that'll teach you to stop looking for issues where there are none." I shrug into my jacket. I introduced them a few years back at a holiday party.

"You could have hinted or something."

"I'm not meddling in your relationship. Jerrick is a good guy, and he loves you."

"Yeah, but after being burned a million times, can you blame me. Fractured hearts have to be handled with care." She shakes her head, waiting as I lock the office doors." So, instead of a surprise engagement party, we're having a Christmas party since he invited all of our family members. He has the venue, people flying in…"

Her words are muffled, and her mouth moves as the answer drops in my head, kindling a new wave of optimism. *I'll propose to Alexandria.*

It's a long shot. But risk comes with my life. We step inside the elevator, and Susan stares at me as if waiting for my response.

"You'll be there, won't you?" She pushes the button for the ground level. The doors close, and the next steps pop up like instant messages.

"I'll be there with bells on because Jerrick will need my support. I've met your family." We laugh as I slide on my gloves. I need a ring and a compelling reason. I could tell Alexandria about the threats. *Hum…* That will only scare her off. I'll keep it simple. She knows about my desire to bring my parents here and the house. "Can you make a few calls on your way out?"

"I don't appreciate you taking shots at my family."

"He is my friend, and in times like this, male solidarity is vital." She rolls her eyes pulling out her cellphone. "I need the house prepared for my family's arrival. We have the basic furnishings, but I need you to schedule the interior designer to add personal touches. I want a Christmas tree and lights, the works. And call my jeweler, I need an engagement ring."

The doors open. I step out into the lobby and realize she's not beside me. I glance back at her with a slack jaw, shocked quiet.

"The car is waiting." I remind her.

"What are you about to do?"

I tug at the cuffs of my jacket with a smile on my face. "Propose to my ex-girlfriend."

"*O*h, no, no, no..." The screaming smoke detector snaps me back to the real world.

I jump up from my paper-covered dining room table running past the agitated device. The dark smoke rising from the oven is the issue.

"Great, Alex, you burnt the biscuits." I yank open the oven, fanning a towel to clear the space in front of my face. The biscuits are not golden brown but charcoal black. I grab an oven mitt, maybe I'll have time to start another batch. Pain shoots through my arm the moment I brush the side of the hot oven. "What is wrong with me?"

I run to the sink and run cold water over the throbbing welt on my arm. I examine my forearm, and it's red, but I'll live. I turn off the water examining the mess I've made.

I never burn food. *Never.* It's one of the few hobbies

I have time for with constant traveling and work. But I couldn't sleep last night and decided to make homemade biscuits instead of the canned ones.

The chime of my phone signals a text message. It's Mateo and simply states, *On my way. See you in twenty.*

"Crap."

I press the timer button off on the stove and retrieve the baking sheet from the floor, tossing it into the sink. I do an awkward bob and weave from side-to-side gathering the black remnants of my buttermilk biscuits.

I have a choice to tidy up my place or put on something more presentable. My oversized Christmas t-shirt and elf striped leggings will have to work. I make quick work of cleaning up my kitchen. By the time I make it back to the table to organize my research, I have ten minutes.

I started researching Mateo, and the more I read, the more I realize I'm in over my head. He's not the same man I knew. I guess some of it must be the same. His habits seem unchanged. He was always a very disciplined person, I can't imagine that changing either, not according to all the facts and figures I found this morning. The man has accomplished the impossible in such a short time.

He arrived as a freshman with a full scholarship. He could read English but didn't speak it fluently, at least not well enough for him to feel comfortable speaking up in class. He endured teasing and professors who doubted him, but his perfect grade point average quieted the most vocal doubters.

Ding dong.

I freeze, looking down the long hall from my dining room table to the front door. My breath catches. What will I say? How will I greet him? I'm stunned the same way he silenced those who felt slighted by the recognition he received.

The film of our relationship flashes in my mind. At one time, Mateo Rodriquez ranked close to oxygen, food, and water. I take several steps, and his silhouette turns from the street to face me as if he can see me.

The naysayers never saw him behind closed doors. That was the man who stole my heart, and he never gave it back. He's the best because he's relentless. Obstacles never stood a chance, and now he's at my home.

I helped him become comfortable with speaking English, and he taught me how to study and embrace the opportunities my family provided. He stressed the need for me to love them. The same people who never gave him a chance or a second thought.

I draw in a deep breath to calm my racing heart and unlock the bolt. My shaky hand grips the brass knob, and I open the door.

"...*mi querida.*" My darling.

Time stands still. This is the moment when you want your ex to look busted, to have suffered without you in their life. But not him. Fucking, sexiness wrapped in a dark suit. Smelling like *do me, baby*.

I start at the top of his jet-black hair stopping only to appreciate his thick lashes and killer bedroom eyes. His strong jaw and tanned skin are precisely the way I remembered. My gaze hovers over his mouth. The same mouth that did wicked things to my body. The slight quiver in his jaw tells me he's struggling to keep his distance.

I rest a hand on my chest, stepping back to let him inside. He crosses the threshold, slamming the door behind him. Then I'm folded into his arms. The musk of his cologne fills my nose, the strength in his arms hold me close, the brush of his lips over my ear renders me mute as desire pulses through my body.

"Alexandria."

I glance up, and the passion lingering in his brandy colored pools overwhelms me.

God, I can't breathe.

His mouth covers mine. Not hot and demanding like the heat I see in his eyes, but it's tender and leisurely as if he's taking his sweet time reacquainting himself with my mouth. The crisp lapels of his suit are crushed in my hands. The kiss slips from tame to demanding to brazen like the man is driving a six-speed, and I'm down for the ride. A delicious shudder shoots through me, I shake it off and reluctantly step away.

Curiosity causes my eyes to sweep the front of his

pants, and the man is hard and ready. There's no way we'll be able to work together. The man looks at me, and I'm willing to let him have his way.

"We can't do that again," I state for the record.

"I don't believe you in your *Santa, I've Been a Bad Girl* shirt." The sexy smile on his face makes my cheeks burn with heat. "Do I get a tour?"

"Uh, yeah, sure." I spin around with him on my heels. "My living room."

I stand back, and he walks over to the picture wall. I have pictures of all my godchildren, the guys, weddings, parties. I have a few of my mother, stepfather, and my siblings. And one with my grandfather when we were inseparable. But most of the wall is dedicated to what I consider my heart family.

"Tell me who I'm looking at."

I make my way across the wall. This is one of the most endearing attributes about Mateo. He loves his family. It was something I envied. But it seems the more I tried to understand my mother, stepfather, and grandfather as an adult, the more I felt like an outcast. That's when I decided to embrace the family I had in the guys.

"From ten, you now have a clan. Look at us." He notices a picture of us from college. He removes it from the wall. The serene smile on his face is infectious. He places it back on the hook turning to me. "How are your parents?"

"They're in good health. Business is good."

"You guys are still distant." He faces me, dropping his hands in his pockets.

"I go when they call, but it's better when we have our own space. Can we talk about something else?"

"Certainly."

The tour continues. My three-bedroom house isn't a mansion, but it's mine. We stop at my dining room table. He glances down at my mess and reaches for a stack of papers.

"I thought I'd prepare for our meeting today. We can talk in here or the living room. I don't have a home office."

"Here is fine." He removes his jacket and my mouth waters. He must be hitting the gym now. "Alexandria, you can't look at me like that and expect me to remain unaffected."

I nod. "Would you like some coffee?"

"I'll get the coffee, and you get the table. Talk me through it."

"Everything is in the drawer below the coffee maker."

He walks in the kitchen spinning around as if getting himself familiar with the space. He stops in front of the coffee maker and pulls out the drawer.

"Bingo." He throws his hands up in a touchdown fashion. I laugh, shaking my head. "Tell me about Platinum Prestige."

"You'd get a kick out of it. We started because

Hunter's father threatened to take away her inheritance. Then he gave her an ultimatum. She created a business plan with her then boyfriend, and when her father agreed to invest in the company, she asked us to join her."

"The mugs?"

"Above you."

He opens the cabinet with his index finger. "Aren't you an organized one?"

"I live on coffee. So, clients work with us on a subscription base. We have celebrities, executives, political officials. We've even started establishing corporate accounts."

"Still two cream, two sugar?"

I stop. "Yes."

He walks to the refrigerator, stopping at the trash can. "What happened?"

"I almost set the place on fire. I got distracted reading about the great Mateo Rodriquez."

"The great? I like the sound of that." His head disappears into the refrigerator. "What are the next steps for Platinum Prestige? You mentioned international expansion."

I sit at the table, watching him move around in my kitchen. He gathers the mugs and strolls into the dining room.

"I guess we'd like to consider duplicating what we've done here in other countries. We currently in the consideration phase. I plan to research and present my findings to the rest of the guys. And we'll take it from there."

"And my role?"

"Do what you do best, advise. Are there particular services we should consider? Should we focus our efforts on the US? How should our financials look before making this type of move? Should we open an international office?" The questions are flowing, and the more I think about it, the more I wonder if we're ready. Having Platinum Prestige based in Austin works for us.

"What's that face about?"

"As I hear myself talk, it makes me think about why our business works in Austin. Eight of our ten partners are married, and all of them have young children. We come and go as needed. It's not easy, but we make it work. I imagine adding an international arm to our business would disrupt that flow."

"It could. But working internationally can take many forms. Are you asking for an evaluation and a recommendation?"

"No, I'd like for you to mentor me."

"Mentor?" His eyebrow creeps up.

"Yes, mentor. I'd like a solid understanding of where we should stand as a company and how I can assist my business partners with this transition. I think handling it in-house could strengthen our structure and give us another level of expertise." I lean forward facing him. "I don't want to be a thirty-year-old intern, but I think I can learn a lot from you. We've exceeded our wildest dreams in the first ten years, I'd love to triple it in another three to five years."

"That's aggressive."

"But we can do it." I'm confident in my team. We've managed to turn trust fund babies into millionaire bosses. The GIB are a formidable powerhouse. It can only go up from here.

"I can help you, Alexandria."

I smile, ready to hug him.

"But…I have a request of my own."

"Okay. And that is?" I search his eyes, trying to anticipate his response.

"Marry me."

CHAPTER 4

"*M*arry you? No… Is this a joke?"

I sit back, reevaluating my approach. In business, I learned the first no is never final. They're usually a knee jerk reaction. I'd be highly concerned if she outright said yes. But I will get a yes.

Alexandria pushes her dark brown hair behind her ears, giving me a full view of her beautiful face. Her plump lips twist in a frown, and I'm not ready to admit defeat.

"Mateo, you can't walk in and propose."

"Would you rather I lie like you did about this boyfriend of yours?" I wait for her response. "The Alexandria I knew wouldn't let me kiss her if she had a boyfriend. Are you the same woman?"

"No, I'm not the same woman. I've changed. That's what time does. You grow up, have mortgages, and stretch the truth *a little*. I don't have a boyfriend, but we can't just start where we left off."

"Says who? Rules serve the creator, not the subject. I create my own rules. Except on this one thing, I need your help." Hesitation lingers in her eyes, but she doesn't look away. I take a deep breath and notice the magazine in question on the table. "You know I was born and raised in Santo Domingo. But I've only returned for holidays since finishing college. I had more opportunities here after graduating, and I see New York as my home—to my parents' dismay."

"You still can't get them to move here?"

She remembers. "No, which is part of the reason for my proposal."

"Okay...I'll listen." She stands up and walks to the kitchen. She pulls out a carton of eggs and a cast-iron skillet. "But this isn't a yes."

I nod, fighting to contain my smile, she sounds like my mother. "My parents have people following them, and earlier this week, they received a nasty threat." I reach for the magazine. "Thanks to this article going into depth about my business and finances."

"A threat?" The clank of the skillet hitting the stove echoes from her quick release.

"I can't get them to move here, but I figure if I can get them here for Christmas, I can hopefully neutralize the situation."

"Why do you have to be engaged to do it?" She leans back against the counter, crossing her arms.

"My mother hates flying. It will take a death, a baby, or a wedding to get her here. She's so ready to marry me off that I'm betting an engagement to you will get her on the plane."

"Why can't you just tell them it's what's best?"

"Did that work when your parents hid the truth about your father?"

"No." Sparks of pain flicker in her eyes before turning away. I stand not stopping until I'm behind her. I wrap my arms around her waist.

"I can't step on my father's toes because he's the man of his house. I can't freak my mother out by telling her the details of the threat. But I won't let my status as a businessman ruin their lives. It's not fair to them, they didn't ask for this."

"I admire your commitment to your family. But what does this have to do with me?"

"You'll buy me a little time. I'm hosting a family Christmas gathering at my place. We'll attend a few Christmas parties. In exchange, I'll mentor you. You'll work in my New York office and get hands-on experience. Then I can help you strategize on a potential rollout approach for Platinum Prestige."

I turn her around to face me.

"Will you please come to New York for the rest of December as my fiancé? That will give me three weeks to have a full security system places on their home. I can hire a detective to investigate the threat. And you can experience a big Dominican Christmas." I used to tell her about them every year. Now, she can experience it for herself.

"How long do you think I'll need to work at your office?"

"Give me six months, and I'll make you a beast in international strategy and negotiations. And I'll have time to introduce you to some vendors with offices in New York."

She sighs. "Start a fresh pot of coffee, and I'll make breakfast."

I step back unbuttoning the cuffs of my sleeves. I roll them back, watching her. Alexandria believes we can't pick up where we left off. But from the looks of things, the core of who we are remains the same. I'm still ready to storm the castle, and she still folds into herself to address the world. It's part of her charm and her flaw. I'd rather make as much noise as humanly possible.

I put on a fresh pot of coffee. I ask for a knife, and she points to the drawer near the refrigerator. I slowly chop the onion and tomatoes. I don't cook, but I'm an excellent sous chef.

In the end, our love was the casualty of her desire to peacefully reach a solution with her family. And in my youth, I chose her happiness over my own. So, I packed up my bags and moved to New York.

I place the bushel of cilantro on the chopping board. "Do you think we would have been married by now had I stayed?"

"You can't ask questions like that." She glances over her shoulder.

"Why not? We didn't break up because of infidelity or because we fell out of love with each other. We were kids trying to figure life out."

"And I let my family drive you away." I hear the slight break in her voice before she returns to scrambling the eggs.

I stop chopping and take a moment to look at her. Her squared shoulders, the hard scrape of the spatula across the skillet, the pain in her eyes. These are all the signs I didn't notice before. I thought leaving was best. Family first is how my parents raised me, and I wasn't family. I couldn't love her and be the source of such pain.

"Was I wrong?" I ask. The smell of fresh spices and bacon fills the air.

"Wrong about what?"

"Leaving you." I lower the knife to the cutting board. "I didn't care that they disliked me. The fact that they didn't know how to cherish you and protect you made me feel responsible for the wedge. I didn't want to be the reason for their callus behavior towards you."

"That's in the past." Her onyx eyes shut me out.

"Not if it keeps us from moving forward.

Was that distance always hidden in her voice? This awakens more questions within me. Questions I didn't consider in my youth like the reason her parents had such strong objections to our relationship. Then I assumed it was the differences in our bank accounts.

Alexandria was born a millionaire. I was born with only my name. I never questioned it further, and she made no attempts to disprove my assumptions. But judging by the tense stance of her posture and her tone, I can't pursue those questions today, not if I want her to let me in.

I MOVE IN HER SILENCE. The light chopping sounds and the sizzle of the bacon are the only indications that I'm not alone. I get a good look around. There's no Christmas tree or lights. The house is deathly silent.

And between kissing her and asking her to marry me, my fake proposal and her real "no" hit on my old insecurities. That I'd never be good enough for her. That I wasn't worth choosing, worth her love. I left, but she never once called me. The threats against my parents and her first phone call to New York brought me back to Austin.

I'm still in love with her.

Shock crashes through me, and I fold forward, thankful her back is turned. I slowly exhale the mounting pressure around my racing heart. I grip the edge of the island as my heavy-lidded gaze examines her profile.

I allow my mind to formulate the real question. Is this

request for her, my parents, or me? It's for me. I'll protect my parents, even if I have to relocate my life back to Santo Domingo. But from the moment I heard her voice, I wanted her back, as this man, not the man I was before.

God, please, give me a second chance to love her, to shower her with all you've blessed me with, to give us a different outcome.

Alexandria glances back as if she heard my prayer. Her eyes probe, holding me captive. I search the depths of her beautiful eyes until I reach her soul, and I know she still loves me too.

Springing a marriage proposal on her, whether fake or real, is shocking. But if this is our opportunity to have Alexandria and Mateo again, it can't happen in Austin. Not with her parents and family around.

The moment comes, and I'm anchored to a truth about us, we once had something special. We'll get it back.

We eat, and I notice the time. "I need to get going. I have a meeting with Liam."

She walks me to the door, and I cup her face in my hands. Her cinnamon-brown skin is as smooth as satin. Her plump lips are covered in gloss. I kiss her once, and once more. I step back from the warmth of her arms and remove the ring from my pocket.

I hold the black dome box between us. The last time I thought about marriage, I was twenty-two years old without a cent to my name. I had nothing to give her but my love and my word. Today, I can give her both and more.

"I bought this for you. The first time I asked you to marry me, I was a kid with a fierce dream. Your parents had every right to question my ability to provide for you. But they were wrong when they thought I wanted their money, your money." I remove the pear cut diamond ring from the box, preparing myself for the fight of my life. Her hands cover her mouth. "I'm asking you to pretend to love me."

"Why me?"

"A man like me should always have a woman like you in his corner." In my heart, I know Alexandria is the missing piece. I take her hand and slide the ring on her delicate finger. I kiss her, thankful she didn't say no and that she leaves the ring on. Now, to get her to say yes. A slip my tongue into the warmth of her mouth, and she moans. We can't fabricate or fake this. And it's my place to help her see. "I have to get going."

Alexandria walks me to the door.

"The flight leaves tomorrow morning at five. All I need is a text from you, and I'll send a car." She opens her mouth and afraid to hear another rejection I kiss her softly. "Just think about it."

I turn and leave after I hear the door lock behind me. And there's a whisper deep inside that wants more than December, more than a ruse to ensure my parents' safety. The next few weeks are all I can ask for, hoping she'll board the flight with me tomorrow.

CHAPTER 5

"*D*ayum, Gina! Ain't nothing fake about that boulder." Charlee's eyes buck then squint rocking my hand from side to side under the direct light from above. The diamond shimmers and the display garners a collective chorus of oohs and awws from round the table.

The moment the door closed behind Mateo, I sent an SOS message to my guys with a picture of the ring he placed on my finger. Now the ten of us are squeezed into a booth at Smith & Jameson with a large order of seasoned fries, several pitchers of beer, and the boulder, as Charlee so eloquently put it.

This is our usual hangout spot. Great food, beer, and music. But we rarely get together for drinks between the husbands and kids. This holiday season it seems harder than the years before as we struggle individually and collectively to nurture our friendships and our business.

"He wants me to stand in as his fiancé for a few holiday parties through the end of the month." I clarify as my hand is passed around like baby Reign.

"And then what sweetie?" Harper asks.

"He agrees to serve as my mentor and help me create a plan for our international rollout if that's what we decide." I pull my hand back into my lap. I glance down, and it's beautiful.

"Will you tell your parents?" Hunter asks.

"It's only for a month."

"Fake or not, don't you think your parents will want to know?" Chase asks.

"No." Hunter, Harper, and Charlee sing in unison.

Chase turns her curious gaze my way. "That sounds like a story."

"Mateo and I dated in college. On the night of our graduation, he asked me to marry him. But my parents didn't approve. So, instead of making me choose between my parents and him, Mateo left. And we haven't talked to each other in over fifteen years until a few days ago."

"Do you still love him?" Ryann leans forward.

"I never stopped loving him. But love wasn't the issue."

"Okay, so, what's the issue?" Ryann's gaze holds mine. She's an attorney. But her past and mine are closer than she realizes. Her father killed her mother, and my biological father was part of the Mexican cartel.

I swallow hard. I've carried this for years. It's time I make some sense of this situation. I look down at the ring again. Plus, I owe him an answer.

"My parents met in college. A story similar to the one I share with Mateo except my parents eloped defying my grandparents once they learned she was pregnant with me. And like you, Hunter," I lock eyes with her, "my grandparents laid down an ultimatum. Antonio Martinez or her family."

"Why would they make her choose between her husband and family?" Harper asks, gathering my hands beneath the table. I glance over and smile through my tears.

"Originally because my father is Mexican." The words scrape out in a hushed whisper hanging between us. Mortification grips my throat. Ashamed and embarrassed, I drop my head. "My Black grandfather forbad my mother from marrying that Mexican man. Is how he put it? And how dare she bring home his wetback baby." Tears sting my eyes. It's the first time I'm vocalizing the source of my torn existence. That's all I've ever been was her mistake.

The tears race down my face, and I can't stop them. "Then, he found a way to separate them. He used his money and power to dig into my father's past. He learned my father's family is connected to the Mexican cartel. My grandfather used that piece of information and his power to get my father promptly deported. I was left to live as the evidence of my mother daring to defy my grandfather's orders."

A chill of numbness tempers my pain. I realize my mother was a victim of her love for my father. A love she let go the way I let Mateo go. What if my grandfather jeopardized Mateo's career?

I couldn't ruin his life. So, I served the penalty of our love I let him go satisfying my grandfather's and my mother's requests.

I twist the ring around my finger, trying to tuck these feelings back in the box. Memories of my grandfather's harsh words and my mother's compliance are the lens that color my entire childhood and my belief that love is conditional. That I had to find a Black man with a professional career, and my family had to approve. Until I found my guys and Mateo.

"That's why I love you guys so much." Pain shoots through my heart, and I fold over, letting my pants collect my tears. The table is moved back, and I'm cocooned in a huddle of love.

"Let it go, sweetie," Harper whispers.

So, I do. My silent cry collides with my buried rage, sending my body into a violent fit of shakes. My battles with isolation, self-hate, and inadequacy have been my constant companions since childhood. My body feels as if it's on fire. But I've learned to not release the slightest whimper because I wouldn't give my mother and grandfather the satisfaction of seeing me break.

The guys hold me until it passes, I sit back, and there's not a single dry eye. Hunter is huddle in front of me with Charlee and Taylor on either side. Ryann and Harper flank me leaving Parker, Jordan, and Payton to enclose our sister circle within a secure embrace.

Makeup is smeared. Noses are runny.

"I pay too damn much for this beer for these hard-ass napkins."

A whisper of silence cuts through our circle before a fit of laughter chases away the pain. I laugh and laugh, falling back in the seat, holding my stomach.

"Charlee, you should be a standup comedian with your crazy ass." Payton chuckles, removing her leather Steel Ryders jacket.

"Speaking of crazy, I think we should make a wish." Jordan peaks through with a dreamy smile on her face. "I know it sounds crazy, but think about it. Each of us found our true loves on holidays. Hunter found Ben on Valentine's Day. Then Harper and Liam on St. Patrick's Day."

"That sexy-ass Irish man."

"Drool over your own husband." Harper swats at Charlee.

"I don't want him. That, my dear, is a fact."

The laughter rolls through us again, and I think about Jordan's words. "So, a Christmas wish?"

"Why not?" Jordan adds. "If I found my prince on Halloween, why can't we all?"

"Because I don't like what my grandfather did to my mother, but if she finds out I'm seeing Mateo again, they'll disown me. It's like she's turned into my grandfather times ten. I won't do that to him."

"So, you're going to decline Mateo's offer?" Hunter asks.

"No, he needs my help." I keep the details private because he didn't give me permission to share them. "I'll accept his mentorship and stay in New York until my task is complete."

"That doesn't sound like a wise plan. You still love the guy." Ryann adds. "I tried to ignore my love for X, and it was useless."

"Sometimes you have to take a chance," Parker adds.

"This is not a chance I'm willing to risk." I think about Mateo's kiss and add for the record. "And I can't sleep with him again. The man kissed me today and…"

"Ahhh, *shyte* now! He had you all hot and bothered?" Charlee does her infamous shoulder shake, and I can't imagine life without this or them.

"Yes, hot, bothered, and horny. But I can't cross that line." I cut through the air.

"That's your decision. You're accepting his proposal…" Hunter says.

"…and the mentorship," Ryann says.

"But, you're keeping your *legs* closed." Charlee sings. "How do you plan to do that? You'll be on his turf.

Mistletoe and snow. Wining and dining. Girl, you better get ready."

Get ready? How? Someone, please tell me how I can resist the man who has me lip-locking within seconds. Perfectly disproportioned lips. The man with a quiet strength I wish I could climb inside and hide, even if for only a moment.

I felt him watching me while I cooked. His eyes assessing me. My body trembling under his overt scrutiny.

I doubt I'll marry. Watching my mother marry her father's older best friend knowing she still loved my father sucked every possible romantic gene from my body. And somewhere down the road, her unhappiness became a direct target on my back, once again leaving me to fend for myself.

My love for Mateo never turned ugly or demanding. Our love lives on in my mind, and it's pretty close to perfect. My greatest fear is that this fake engagement will trade my happiest memories for ones that resemble the men I've known in my life.

Men like my father, who left and never returned. Like my grandfather, who uses his money and power to throw his weight around.

I'd rather die than to lump Mateo with the likes of them, so a part of me would rather hold on to the fantasy than risk it. That's why I can't give him my body. I won't deprive myself of his kisses. But making love to him will muddy our obviously complicated situation.

I roll my shoulders back, suppressing my groan. How did I get myself into this situation? My guys.

They work together to straighten the tables. I'll risk entangling myself with Mateo to take our business dreams to the next level and because I want us to succeed. For every million I make on my own, I show my grandfather and my mother that I don't need them or their money.

After an emotional evening, we decide to head out to the courtyard and order more than fries from one of the food trucks. I follow the gang pulling out my phone.

I send Mateo a quick text, *I accept.*

CHAPTER 6

"*I*'m impressed." Alexandria cuddles beneath a quilt.

I wag my head, rubbing my eyes. The soothing hum of the engine has me fighting to stay awake. Her late-night text set the wheels of this Christmas celebration in motion. The moment I mentioned the engagement and Alexandria's name, my mother magically forgot about her fear of flying. Now, Alexandria and I are flying to New York, and my family is flying in tomorrow. And Susan is demanding a raise for coordinating it all.

"Would you like a drink, something to eat, a kiss?" My head drops to the seat, and I glance over at Alexandria.

"No, but I'd like to know what I'm walking into."

I shrug. "We have an engagement party slash

Christmas party to attend this evening for Jerrick and his fiancé, Susan, who is also my executive assistant."

"Jerrick lives in New York too?"

"Yep, he moved with me and stayed. He's president of a software development company. I'm trying to woo him back to my team, but he refuses."

"Keep business business and personal personal." She does an excellent impression of Jerrick's motto.

"Exactly." My eyelids flutter under the weight of exhaustion. "Tomorrow, we'll have a large family dinner and a traditional installing of a Nacimiento."

"Nacimiento? What's that?"

"You would consider it the nativity scene. It's the center of our Christmas celebration." I cover a yawn. "Since I only got them to agree to visit for one week, we'll adhere to the regular Christmas dates. The kids open their gifts on Christmas Eve, and we'll have a huge Dominican party all night. The adults will wear ugly sweaters and exchange white elephant gifts. You'll have a blast."

"How many people are you expecting?"

"Close to fifty, maybe a few more."

"Fifty! I thought you said it's a family party."

"It is, but family includes everyone. Did you pack an ugly sweater?"

"No, I brought party clothes. You didn't tell me."

"Don't worry. We'll get it. I still need to get gifts for the gift exchange. I hope you're ready because it's going to be a long week. The house will be full of kids, family,

Christmas cheer, and mistletoe." My eyes close, and I let the peace of knowing everyone will be under my roof tomorrow wash over me. I catch myself before sleep takes me under. I glance over at Alexandria. "Thank you."

"You're welcome. But I haven't done anything yet. Tired?" Her eyes caress my face, and I brush my thumb over her kissable lips.

"Yeah. I worked through the night." I request coffee from the stewardess and drop my hands in my lap. I must resist her tempting skin and lips and eyes. I have to show her why we work. Somewhere while planning flights and having the house prepared, I decided I want more than December. Now, to convince Alexandria. And my plan is simple, show her with love. I drop my hand to her knee. "How are you?"

The smile slips from her face. "I'm nervous about meeting your parents, especially your mother. What if she doesn't like me?"

"Don't be. You have a lot in common."

"Like what?" She turns in the chair, gathering her knees to her chest.

"Cooking. Except she doesn't burn her Jonnycakes." Her jaw goes slack, and laughter pours from me. She chuckles and tosses a crumpled napkin at me.

"You should do that more often. I always loved your laugh." A smile lightly brushes her lips, and I want to kiss her again.

"Love is a strong word, *mi querida*." Yesterday's kiss

awakened the vivid images of the years we spent together. The feel of her beneath me, the feeling of being inside her.

"Turn off the charm Mateo, tell me about your mother."

"Pushy, pushy. Is this more of your boundaries talk?"

She giggles. "Yes, now talk."

"She loves cooking and quilting. Oh, she loves practicing her English, thanks to me telling her about you."

"Me?" Her hand rests on her chest as if in shock.

"I never lied to my mother about my love for you. So, practice with her while she's visiting. She speaks well."

"You do, as well. I'm proud of you."

"Thank you. I had an amazing tutor. Now can I get that kiss?" I close my eyes, puckering my lips.

Her hands feather up the sides of my face until her fingers comb through my hair. The sound of her shifting closer causes heat to stir through my body. I open my eyes, watching her lean over the armrest, resting her full breasts on my chest.

I circle an arm around her waist. Our eyes hold, then her mouth brushes mine with a sweeping motion before her tongue traces the crease between my lips. The smooth slip of her tongue is fucking hot.

I cup her ass in my hand, massaging it until I hear her moan. The expert teasing, licking, and petting sends shock waves through me. How could I forget how she loves foreplay?

I wiggle my hands beneath her blanket, brushing the peaks of her nipples, listening for her groan of approval. I hear the door to the stewardess bay open and reluctantly release her tempting mouth.

She sits back in her seat. We share an electrifying gaze. I watch the rapid rise and fall of her chest as my coffee is placed on the tray. Then we're left alone.

"I have a small request for this fake engagement of ours." She sits forward, opening the creamer and sugar packets, pouring it into my cup.

"And that is?"

"No sex."

A WIDE SMILE crawls across Mateo's face.

"Did you hear me?"

He brushes a hand over the exposed flesh above the collar of my shirt. A shiver of awareness makes my kitten leap anxious to sample more than his kisses. But Mateo will have me screaming the plane down and ready to throw caution to the wind. But I can't, not with the thought of my family lingering in my mind. I can't risk it.

"Yeah."

"I'm serious, Mateo. Sex will complicate it. Promise me. No sex."

"Even if you beg for it."

"Beg?" I lick my lips, tasting him.

"Beg." The word is laced with a challenge matching the sexual fire in his eyes.

"I've never begged a day in my life."

He taps his temple as if calling on a memory. "Your birthday, junior year."

Against my will and good sense, my mind takes me back to that night, and a wildfire spreads through my body. I clench my thighs tight. This is why I can't. Sex with him was never just sex. It was an escape from my reality, medicine for my ails, a refuge when I needed...*him.*

"Okay, ...okay...that one time. Damn, stop bringing up old stuff."

Mateo's head falls back, and I laugh with him, trying to mask the kernel of fear. Hunter is right. I am a different person with him. I drop my head on his shoulder.

"I think this will be the best Christmas ever." He places a soft kiss on my forehead.

"Yeah, I think so too."

I have to tread lightly, or I'll find myself falling back *in* love with him again.

CHAPTER 7

*T*he chauffeured car drives through the Upper East Side of New York. I look up at the concrete building and back at Mateo.

"You live in a condo?"

He shakes his head. "The penthouse."

The driver opens his door, and Mateo slips out. I look back at the building, counting to the sixth floor, confused. "Penthouse?"

He opens my door, and I take his offered hand. "Give us two hours, and I'll take the luggage inside."

"Yes, Mr. Rodriquez." The driver pulls away from the curb, and I survey the street. The neighborhood seems quiet. There are similar units down both sides of the road. They resemble townhomes to me. But I've never seen a six-story townhouse.

"Welcome home!" A petite, plump woman with

short brown hair is at the top of the steps with her arms opened wide. Mateo takes the stairs two at a time and swoops her up into a bear hug. He makes loud kissing noises on her cheeks, and she swats at each one.

He lowers her to the ground, and her attention turns to me. I climb the stairs standing beside him.

"Tia Marie, I'd like to introduce you to my fiancé Alexandria Martinez."

I tense, my eyes seek his. His response is a slight lift of his eyebrow. *Game on*.

"Why didn't you tell me?" She playfully swats at his arm. Her eyes radiate with excitement. "It's about time, Mateo. To think you've worried your poor mother. Wait until I tell her."

"You don't have to wait long...she'll be here tomorrow. Surprise."

Her hand covers her heart in stunned silence. Her lips quiver, and she starts crying. I know it's from happiness because her smile is so serene.

"Tia Marie is my mother's sister." He tells me.

"The one you lived with when you moved here?" I recall.

"Yes." He gathers Marie in his arms, her head rests on his chest. She's wiping away the tears, but they keep falling. "They haven't seen each other since she moved to the States." He places a soft kiss on her forehead.

"Nice to meet you, Marie." I reach in my purse and pass her a tissue.

"Please call me Tia Marie." She sniffles. "It's wonderful to finally meet you too. Let's get you inside and settled in."

Tia Marie guides us inside. Mateo closes the door behind us, and I'm blown away.

"Take her luggage upstairs, and I'll give her the tour." She guides me forward, and I'm ready to see every inch of the house.

"We only have one-hour, Tia," Mateo calls from behind us.

"We'll be back."

The entry floor is the family area. A living room, formal dining room, kitchen, family room, and several bathrooms. The decor is modern and sleek. The monochromatic color scheme in shades of gray moves from room to room, but each has a different accent color. The tour is quick, but I notice black, teal, and red.

"We can take the stairs or the elevator."

"Elevator?" I turn around, and Tia Marie is waiting by a single door elevator. "So, this building is one house."

"Si. I'll show you my floor, and we'll see the others tomorrow." We take the stairs. "I stay on this floor to keep an ear on the house."

"You live here?" I ask.

"Uh, huh. It's how Mateo wanted it."

He did it. He told me he'd do it and he did. The

sprawling mansion is beyond impressive. Tia Marie's "floor" is a full apartment with a living room, bedroom, one and a half bathrooms, and a kitchen. Her decor is vibrant, and it feels like a home reflecting her jovial energy.

I stop looking at her magnificent view.

"Welcome to New York, sobrina."

My heart warms at her calling me niece. "Thank you, Tia Marie."

"Let me show you my favorite room."

She walks with a bounce in her step, and I follow to the back room. She opens the door stepping aside, and I enter a sewing room. I stand in the middle and turn a tight circle.

"You're a quilter."

"And do you remember this?"

She walks over to a closet and removes a blanket. She peels back the folds, and I can't see through my tears. "He kept it."

"No, chica, he killed it."

We laugh as I gather the quilt to my chest. It's the first quilt I made, and he insisted on keeping it. I run my hands over the unraveling seams.

"I wasn't very good then," I admit.

"We never are in the beginning. Now let's get you back downstairs."

I gather the quilt to my chest, inhaling Mateo's scent. I fold it gently and set it on a side table.

"You can come and sew anytime," she offers, closing the door behind us.

"I plan to take you up on that offer."

We take the elevator back down, and I can't believe he still has that quilt. We stumbled on a small quilt shop in Austin one weekend, and as a Christmas gift, he bought me a gift certificate to a beginner's class. I went with my little Singer machine from Walmart.

"Are you okay, chica?"

"Yes, ma'am. That quilt brings back good memories."

"It does for you both."

The bell rings and the doors open, and Mateo is sitting on his cellphone.

"Thank you for the tour." I face her with the blanket still on my mind.

"You're welcome. It feels good to finally put a face with a name. We'll have more time to sit and get acquainted during your visit." She hugs me, and it's strong and filled with love. "Welcome to the family." She whispers before letting me go.

Family. The word lingers long after she rides the elevator back to her apartment, and Mateo ushers me out to the waiting vehicle. And for a moment, I wonder how his family will respond when they learn this engagement is a ruse.

. . .

"MADISON AND 57TH," Mateo calls to the driver, and the SUV pulls into the flow of traffic.

I sit back, keeping an ear on Mateo's phone calls and my eyes on the city. Tia Marie's tour of the "family mansion" was once a dream for Mateo, to have all of his family under one roof.

She told me the basics. It's actually seven stories, four of which are similar to her apartment. Then there's a family game room in the basement. The top two floors are Mateo's penthouse apartment. The driver returned, and now we're making a mad dash into the city for a little shopping.

"We don't have to do this now," I whisper, glancing over at him. He lifts the armrest between us, placing a hand on my leg. His long fingers wrap my thigh, and our eyes hold.

"We're fine. Susan usually handles this, but tonight's her big night." He explains, and for the next fifteen minutes, I listen as Mateo manages to open several high-end boutiques with a call.

"I'd like to stop and get them a gift."

"We got them one." He says, dropping the phone in his pocket as the SUV rolls to a stop.

"What did *we* get them?"

"A seven-day honeymoon to a destination of their choice." He opens the door and disappears, leaving me alone for only a second to process his statement. He helps me out, tucking my hand around his arm, and like before the doors open to greet us.

"Mr. Rodriquez, Miss Martinez, please have a seat, and I'll bring out a few of our best selections." A chic woman motions with a flourish of her hand to a couch.

"Huh, okay," I respond, eyeing Mateo.

"I'm Galiana. Welcome to my boutique. Tell me, do you like short or long. Fitted or flowing."

I answer the questions, and a small army starts moving around, pulling dresses, accessories, shoes. Mateo makes phone calls stopping periodically to offer suggestions for alterations or color changes.

"I can't try on another stitch of clothing," I demand exhausted after over an hour of quick changes. I'll have to tape my eyes open tonight.

"Galiana, charge my account and deliver everything to the house. I want the red gown, with the shoes and accessories delivered here within an hour." He gives her a card.

"Yes, sir. Thank you." Galiana gives me a set of air kisses, and I'm whisked away.

This repeats for four more boutiques, and I'm looking at him, stunned. "Mateo, this is overwhelming. There's no way I'll wear all of these formal gowns and dresses in this lifetime."

"I always wanted to do this." He kisses me, and I kiss him back. "I remember when we used to share a pizza buffet. When I gave you a single ornament for Christmas. Let me spoil you, *mi querid*a."

I nod. In college, I didn't want to use my parents' money, and Mateo couldn't work as a stipulation of his scholarship. We struggled together, neither of us complaining.

The final stop is at a spa. He requests the works from head to toe, and with a parting kiss, Mateo disappears.

CHAPTER 8

*A*lexandria steps into the lobby, and I only see her. I stand to my feet as our eyes hold for what feels like a lifetime. We talked about shopping in New York, traveling the world, gowns, yachts, and cars. But none of our wishing sessions felt like this.

I'm breathless, heart-pounding, fingers burning with the compulsion to touch her. And my heart whispers, *mine.*

Her caramel skin wrapped in a Christmas red dress like a gift, specially created for me. The imported fabric follows the peaks of her breast, valleys of her small waist, and contour her full hips falling into a pool of layers at her feet. Her hair is styled off her neck, and the diamonds sparkle across her chest. We're running late, but I'd rather take her home and unwrap my present.

The click of her heels brings her closer, I swirl my finger, and she does a sexy spin. The rocking of her hips causes my eyes to settle on her sweet bottom. She stops glancing back over her shoulder, she winks, then completes the rotation. I trace a finger down the hollow of her cheek and brush a kiss over her lips.

"You look absolutely gorgeous, *mi querida*."

"Thank you. I have to keep up with you in this tuxedo. I'll have to beat them off with a stick."

I kiss the inside of her neck, her soft moan encourages me to kiss up until my lips hover over her diamond-studded ear. "Not with my rock on your finger."

"Especially with this boulder on my finger. You gave Tia Marie quite a shock with your announcement. How will you handle your friends?"

I chuckle, loosening my grip as she snuggles closer. "You have nothing to worry about, as for my friends, my friends will be told. Others will have to fill in the blanks."

"Have you considered your explanation once I head back to Texas?"

"How about we enjoy the evening and let the future handle itself?"

She cuts me a glare, smoothing her hands up the lapels of my jacket. "This place is heaven on earth."

"It's at your disposal." I release a long exhale, thankful for the shift transition. This is moving at the speed of lightning. First the idea, then the ring and proposal, and now she's here in my arms. "We need to get going before I send our regrets and take you home."

She steps back. "Oh no, you don't. Not after all this work. Take a picture for my guys."

Alexandria passes me her phone. Through the phone screen, I appreciate her beauty, the way her hand rests delicately on her waist, the seductive pucker of her lips, and the twinkle in her eyes. I snap several pictures for her and one for me. I removed her coat for my arm and drape it over her shoulders. "Bundle up, it's freezing out there."

"Where's the engagement party?" I help her button-up and wrap a thick scarf around her neck, careful not to disturb her hair.

"A few blocks up at the Four Seasons."

She yawns, drawing my attention to her mouth. "I hope I make it. It's been a crazy long day, and after that massage, I can barely keep my eyes open."

"We'll stop by and make an appearance. Then get you into bed." I emphasize bed, and her eyes darken with lust. Her little rant about no sex echoes in the back of my mind. But the Alexandria I knew could stay in bed for days, only stopping to eat, sleep, and shower.

I bundle her up, and we make the short trip. People stop and stare the moment we enter the lobby of the hotel. It's all her doing, she commands the attention of all. The click of her heels, the sway of her hips, the dramatic sting of diamonds provides a striking display of royal beauty.

And she's with me. I pause, pulling her back against me.

Her eyes round at the sudden movement, her flirty smile makes me wish I had her alone. "Mateo…"

I have to taste her, not giving a damn about her sticky lip gloss, or the people standing around. This kiss is tender and slow. She steps back after wiping her gloss off my lips.

"Thank you." I know she feels the chemistry between us. But will she trust it?

"Don't thank me yet, handsome. I might have you on the dance floor all night." She looks over my shoulder towards the base bumping from up ahead.

We follow the music until we're standing in the reception hall. Jerrick spots us the moment we enter. He flags down Susan, and they walk in our direction.

I introduce Alexandria and Susan. Then Jerrick, in his true fashion, folds Alexandria in a brotherly hug. I give Susan our gift and kiss her cheek. "Congratulations."

"Thank you. And this has you written all over it." Susan says, side-eyeing him. "Jerrick would have had us at the house eating barbecue."

I make the sign of zipping my lips.

"Does it matter?" Jerrick asks. "Your man came through, that's all that matters. Right?"

"Right." She rolls her eyes and mouths, *Barbecue*.

Alexandria laughs, and I help her remove her jacket.

"I'll introduce her around while you tell Jerrick how much he owes you for handling the party," Susan smirks, dragging Alexandria in the opposite direction.

"Did you tell her?" I ask the moment they disappear.

"No, I thought you did. Man...that's scary. She's already acting like a wife. I'm not sure whether I should be excited or scared right now." Jerrick shakes his head in disbelief.

I laugh. Susan's right, as usual. I had my event planner handle everything. Except Jerrick doesn't owe me a dime, I'm happy to cover tonight's festivities. And my gift-giving will be officially handled after tonight.

"You think she saw the invoice?" Jerrick asks, scratching across his low-cut fade.

"No, she just knows stuff. It's a woman thing and why my life runs seamlessly." I watch Alexandria and Susan dart from one end of the room to the other.

"So, you and Alex back doing y'all thang?"

I nod towards the door. I see Alexandria and Susan talking to a group of women. We slip out into the hallway. "I proposed to her."

He stares at me tongue-tied. "To Alex? What? Did I miss something?"

"No. She agreed to pretend to be my fiancé through the end of the month."

"Only you would think of something ridiculous as a

fake fiancé. What did you have to do to get her to agree?" His eyes squint suspiciously.

"That's between us."

"And how will you let her go again once the month is over?"

"I'm sort of hoping she'll stay." I'm slipping down an oil-slick slope with her. But I can't stop it, and I don't want to. Why fight it?

"And if she doesn't?"

"She will." I meet his direct gaze. It's best to change the subject because I'm not letting her go. "You guys should come by for dinner tomorrow. My folks are flying in for Christmas."

"You're telling your mother about this fake fiancé business?" His says louder than I'd like.

"Man, please talk a little louder the city of New York would love to participate in this *private* conversation." I glance around, ensuring we don't have an audience.

"Your mother will start planning the baby shower. Watch. All I can say is, don't do it."

I shake my head. "Wasn't it you who begged Susan to marry you?"

"Man...you promised to never speak about that night."

"My bad." I cough to disguise my laughter. I swallow hard, fighting to keep a straight face.

"Aw, man... That's how you do me?" His hands are

open in surrender. "You're supposed to be my boy. You out here clowning me." His face drops.

I can't hold it any longer. I burst out laughing.

"She had you begging harder than James Brown." I heave for air. My side is cramping, but it keeps flowing out the more he stands there with that stupid look on his face. "Please baby baby baby please."

"You foul man."

I wipe the tears from my eyes. I stretch back, trying to relieve my stomach.

"Laugh, all you want. I wasn't losing my woman for nothing."

"I know. But that was funny as hell."

We sober up, turning back to the celebration. He wanted to move in together before getting married, and Susan wasn't having it. She returned his ring and told him to lose her number. I knew she was over it the moment she told me, "I'm a wife, and I'm not waiting around for him to recognize it." I did everything but tell him, but he didn't catch my hints.

That was the first time I truly understood the weight of marriage for some women. Alex and I always talked like marriage was inevitable until her parents arrived at her place unexpectedly and found me living there.

"Mateo, if you ever trusted your boy…trust me now. Don't tell your Mom."

I look into my best friend's eyes. "It's too late. She already knows. It was the only way to get them here."

"Just remember I warned you. Now, let's get back inside and enjoy this expensive food you've provided."

I laugh, following him into the banquet hall. It's two halls combined into a sprawling layout. The DJ booth is on the far left with the dance floor covers the center. The right side has circle tables for eating and socializing. The food and open bar line the back wall.

They have a great turnout. I take a deep breath and try to ignore Jerrick's response.

The DJ has the vibe right, and I spot Alexandria from the back. I leave Jerrick talking with some family members making my way across the room. The slight sway of her hips to the music quickens my pace until I'm standing behind her.

"Dance with me," I whisper across her ear, smelling the floral scent of her skin.

"I'd love to."

The moment we boarded the plane, she seemed to relax. I lace our fingers, leading her to the dance floor. I find a clear spot and face her.

My eyes lazily enjoy the sight of her from head to toe. Her petite height brings her head just over my shoulders. I turn her in a full circle then pull her into my arms just as the lights lower to a soft haze. A Jamaican slow wind starts, and she catches the beat with a seductive rock of her hips.

Alexandria loves to dance. She used to dance all night until her feet were sore, and I had to carry her home. I follow her lead, and her side to side rock brings our bodies closer, our eyes lock. Her breast against my chest, my hands wrapped around her. She melts against me, our legs sandwich in a sexual grind. I brush my lips across her shoulder and up her neck, inhaling and exhaling in tandem as a bead of sweat trickles down my spine.

The DJ changes the record. The *boom tat, boom tat* of the base shifts. We dip and roll as the singer cries about a man's lack of love. I spin Alexandria around until her ass molds to my body. I can't disguise my aroused state, her hands grip my thighs like handlebars, throwing her ass back like she's riding my dick. When her smoky eyes glance up, I'm fucking done.

I hold on enjoying my woman and the music, lost in the moment until thunderous applause pulls us out of a seductive trance.

The DJ spins a new record, and each song takes us further down the path of desire. I smell her arousal, the heat rising from her skin, and by the time we climb in the waiting car, Alexandria is straddling my lap. The red fabric drapes around us like a canopy.

I close the privacy window as her sweet heat brushes against my rock-hard flesh, straining under my tuxedo pants. Her hands pass through the layers of fabric between us. I lower the neckline of her dress. I blink mesmerized by the sight of her bare breasts, and she yanks my zipper down.

Her hot little hands wrap around my throbbing cock, and I groan, placing one of her chocolate nipples in my mouth. Her head falls back, stroking my flesh as I feast on her, squeezing her ass, trying to ignore the mounting tension. But her expert hands are about to send me over the edge. And I'm not going alone.

I push back the layers brushing across her damp curls, and I dip inside. Her tormented moan fills the vehicle.

"I thought you said no sex, *mi alma*."

"This isn't sex, Mateo. It's foreplay." Her fist is pumping from the tip of my head to the base of my dick, and I see stars.

"So, me, palm deep in your sweet pussy isn't sexing you?"

"*Got damn you...*" she screams.

I laugh but ain't shit funny. "I almost forgot you like for me to talk to that pussy."

The passionate woman I once craved and love is front and center. The night is cold, the ground is covered in snow, and the city passes in a blur. She's beating my shit, and I'm fighting the inevitable, thrusting so deep in her that my hand is covered in her juices. I press my thumb against her jewel and slip in another finger, and it's lights out.

She's trembling, her nails digging into the side of my neck.

"Papi's home."

Her screams rattle my soul, as her demanding kisses piece me back together. I'm afraid the driver will think

I'm killing her as her final strokes send me over the edge. Both of us dying a little for a sample of heaven.

I growl spent, snaking my free hand up the side of her neck. I bring her mouth to mine.

"Matty, we ruined a ten-thousand-dollar dress."

"I'll buy you another one."

CHAPTER 9

J wake in an unfamiliar bed, in an unfamiliar room, naked. My last memory of last night was seeing Mateo pulling the covers over me. The red dress is tossed across a chair, and I smell Mateo's scent on the pillow beside me. I'm in his bed.

My stomach growls at the scent of seasoned beef in the air.

"Matty." My eyes fall back closed when I hear laughter. I push my head up from the pillow, looking towards the sound. "Mateo."

I sit up, draping the sheet around my body. He walks in with a smile on his face closing the door behind him. He's wearing a pair of pajama pants with no shirt. The man is chiseled with each movement his defined muscles flex until he reaches the bed.

"Good morning." The knowing smile on his face makes me ache for a repeat. He brought my body to completion three times without having to remove a single stitch of clothing.

"Don't you say a word," I warn as embarrassment burns my cheeks. I was a wild woman last night.

"I'm not complaining." He teases sitting on the bed, then he kisses me. I lean in closer for another one and sit back. "How'd you sleep?"

"Like a baby, except I'm starving." My stomach decides to add its two cents, and he laughs. "That is so embarrassing."

"I'll make you a plate. Anything you don't eat?"

"Nah. I'll eat just about anything that's well done and seasoned." I toss my legs over the side of the bed. "Which way is the restroom?"

"That way." He points to the door in the far corner. "Your bags are in the closet, and Galiana had the clothes delivered this morning."

I pivot and head in the direction of the closet. His boisterous laughter fills the air. "Food. Sex. Shopping."

"...are all a woman needs." I enter the closet. It was our running joke. I turn and recognize my sweater. My clothes are hung on the left side. "Did you do this?"

He pops his head around the corner. "Tia Marie."

"Matty..." I whine. "You can't have her doing that. I can take care of myself."

"I'm not telling her that." He throws his hands up.

"She'll think I'm a bum."

"No, she won't. It's her way of saying welcome." Mateo steps inside, closing the door behind him.

"Sweetheart, you must remember you're my fiancé. So, get ready for my family to wait on you hand and foot." He pulls me against his warm body.

"I don't know." I shake my head, uncomfortable with the thought. I'm used to taking care of myself.

"It's the perks of having a big family." He nibbles on my shoulder. "Now get dressed, my folks are waiting to meet you."

"Folks? They're here?" I step back. "When were you going to tell me this?"

"After you put on some clothes." He reaches for my breast, and I smack his hand away. "You're so selfish. You have two."

"Out!" I laugh, pointing at the door. I need to shower, and then I think about my hair. I hurry to the mirror. I jerk my body around a freestanding structure, stopping in front of a wall mirror. I groan at the sight.

"Alexandria…."

"Look at me!" My hair is doing some sort of ridiculous wave, standing straight up in the air. Last night the beautician used all types of hairspray and gel to tame my thick natural curls. Did I even pack shampoo?

He's standing over my shoulder, obviously not understanding the severity of this situation.

"It'll be fine. Just jump in the shower and hurry before everyone eats the food. Mom made la bandera."

"Everyone…"

"Yeah, Mom...Dad...Alejandro..." He rattles off a list of names. "They're staying here."

"Here?" My stomach drops to my feet. I was okay with telling his parents to get them here. But it sounds like his entire family. "That was like a thousand people." I all but yell, and the walls start to close around me.

His strong hands grip my shoulders. "Take a shower. Get dressed. I'll be back in fifteen minutes."

"Make it ten." I pull down a pair of jeans and grab a sweater. They must know I'm in here. I spin around, looking at the row of shoes and spot mine on the end. I scurry over and pick up my sneakers. I need underwear. I spin back and see the island with drawers. "It's like I live here already."

"I designed it as a his and her closet."

"More like an efficiency apartment," I mumble, opening a few drawers until I recognize the fabrics inside. I grab panties, a bra, and some socks. I'm holding the sheet in one hand and the clothes with my other making my way back to the bedroom. "What time is it?"

"One thirty."

A wave of dizziness passes over me. His aunt put away my clothes. His mother cooked. And I had my lazy ass in the bed until two o'clock. Fake fiancé or not, I'm making a bad first impression, and I haven't met them yet. I take long drags, trying to force air into my lungs.

"Why...why...why...did you let me?" I fold over,

trying to make the room stop swaying. I notice the slits in my jeans. "I can't wear these. They'll think I'm a slut."

I turn to find something else, and Mateo scoops me up into his arms. I wiggle and swing my arms, trying to free myself as he stalks out of the closet and lays me on the bed. The sheet is pulled away, the clothes are tossed aside, and he settles between my legs.

"Stop it, Alex." Determination shines in his eyes. "You had a long day yesterday. They understand."

"I'm fine." I lie, struggling to hear his words over my heart. I'd rather stay in the closet than meet his family like this. I can only imagine what they're thinking.

I look away. A life of being the wrong child, the wrong skin color, the wrong father, makes perfectionism my comfort zone. Sluts that lounge around in bed all day miss the mark by a mile.

Mateo adjusts his weight, squirming down my body. "You should always be covered in diamond *mi querida.*" His kisses run the length of my collarbone as if sampling the flavor of each diamond.

"No…you can't." I try to hold him still by squeezing my thighs around his waist.

"Shh…or, my mother will hear you." He laughs.

"I don't see what's so damn funny." I push to sit up, and my hands are stretched above my head, and my breast is in his mouth. The suckling motion and the twirl of his tongue quiet my protests. He unlatches and hovers over me, eye to eye.

"What do you require, *mi querida*? As long as my

ring is on your finger, this is your home. That is your family. I am your man. You're safe and loved here."

His words are killing me. Every run-in with my family, every disappointment, he'd remind me that I was safe, and I was loved. I close my eyes, shaking my head.

This is all pretend. I'm not his fiancé, and even if his words of love are real, my family will never accept him.

"I'm okay," I swallow hard and meet his gaze.

"You don't have to lie to me."

"Just give me fifteen minutes, and I'll be right out." I force my lips to smile, internally pleading for him to believe me.

"I'll give you ten."

I sigh in relief as he pushes back into a sitting position. I reach for the sheet and quickly gather my clothes with his eyes watching my every move. I glance back before reaching the bathroom, and the intensity of his gaze causes me to stumble. I rush inside and close the door.

"Damn." I scan the bathroom. Double vanities on either side of me lead to a large bathtub. The shower occupies the far corner behind glass panels. I walk closer, and the showerhead is a large square hanging from the ceiling. Are those light bulbs or cameras? I squint, trying to get a better look.

I open the door and get my answer. Blue lights flick

on, and I hop back. The lights turn off. I hop forward, and the lights turn on again. I smile. Must be a motion detector.

I play with digital display and get the water going. I step out to let it the water warm up. I see Mateo's hygiene products to the left, so I head to the vanity on the right.

I drop the sheet and remove the diamond necklace and the studs. I unfasten the diamond bracelet and slip off my engagement ring. When did I become this woman? Not the one dripping in diamonds but the one so concerned about the opinions of everyone. Even Mateo.

I scrub my scalp with the pads of my fingers searching for any remaining bobby pins, and once I'm satisfied that they're all removed, I climb in the shower. I tilt my head back, letting the water cover me.

The truth is, I lost a piece of myself when I let my family run Mateo out of my life. In my attempts to protect the love we had, I became a shell of myself until Hunter started Platinum Prestige. That was my first real step towards independence from my family.

It's time to decide what I want now and for my future.

The shower door opens, and Mateo steps inside. The steam swirls around us. I let my eyes caress the lean lines of his body. The definition in his chest, six-pack, and arms.

"What's that?"

"Shampoo and conditioner. I took them from Tia's bathroom. Turn around."

I obey, keeping an eye on him. His tight butt and the growing state of his erection. He sits a bottle on the bench and opens the other.

"You can't keep staring at it, love."

I giggle. "But, it's cute."

"No man, what's his dick called cute. Now, turn around." Our laughs echo, and I turn my back to him. "Do you remember the first time I washed your hair?"

He separates my hair dropping one side over my shoulder. I hold it looking up.

"Do I? I had to cut chunks out of my hair from all the tangles. I can laugh at the memory now, but then I wanted to kill him."

"I thought it was a romantic gesture before we had to get the scissors. You gave me a long lecture about Black women and their hair." He chuckles. "Tilt your head back." I close my eyes, enjoying the feel of his large hands massaging my scalp, slowly raking through my curls.

"I can finish it."

"I know. But I figure we'll either turn into raisins or you'll talk to me." He makes quick work of adding the conditioner.

"What about your family?" I plait the section, and he moves to the other side.

"What about them?" I open my mouth and find myself caged against the glass. "Remember I'm the man that slept in the same bed with you for two years. Four years of knowing a person adds up."

"Okay, I'm done."

"No, we're not, not then or now. What will it take for you to see that?"

"This is not why I came here. You asked for my help. I helped you. Now, move."

Mateo takes a step back. The water pounds against his body, his eyes darken with emotion. The personal feelings I tucked away are threatening to spill over. I feel weak and vulnerable, and undeserving. I step out of the shower without a towel aroused by his nearness, disgusted by my response.

The heat of his eyes follows me. I'm starting to think this is a bad idea.

CHAPTER 10

"*M*amá, Alexandria Martinez. Alexandria, my mother, Gloria Rodriquez." My mother covers her shocked response well.

"Alexandria...Martinez. Nice to meet you." She extends a hand, and Alexandria accepts with a tight smile.

Tia Marie is standing nearby, puzzled by the interaction as well. I made the rest of the introductions, and that was the start of our holiday festivities. Alexandria won't talk to me, and I feel blindsided by this invisible thing between her and my mother. It's been days of them bouncing around each other, and today I finally got my mother alone. We're waiting for the interior designer to arrive with the design books for their floor of the house.

"What is it, Mamá?"

"You didn't tell me she was Black," her voice holds a bitter tone.

"I didn't know I had to. She's Mexican and African American. Why does it matter?"

The elevator rings, and the door opens.

"Now I see why her grandfather wanted you away from his granddaughter," she says, the words linger with an air of distaste.

I turn to her, confused. "What does one have to do with the other?"

"You're Dominican, and she's Black." Her chopped English transitions to smooth Spanish in a hushed whisper as the decorator fidgets with her materials. "I thought it was odd for you to date for years and suddenly poof, she was gone. Now, it makes perfect sense. That man didn't want you marrying her. He'd rather pay you off and move you out of the state than let you have her. What will he say now?"

I look away, thinking about my mother's words. I can't respond because her grandfather doesn't know that she's in New York with me. The old man is still running her life. She's still letting him. It was a vicious cycle then, and its worst now because I'm not a boy anymore. I'm a man in command of my life and my business. And now my mother springs this on me. I can't refute your words because a part of me always wondered.

The interior designer takes over, and I leave them alone. I'm paying a mini fortune for the designer to work over the holidays and the security crew in Santo Domingo to fully outfit my parents' home. Aiming to buy myself more time, I thought having the space personalized would help them feel at home. But it seems it's not enough because they're still set on leaving the day after Christmas.

My parents have a floor like Tia Maria, and my siblings share the final level beneath mine. I ride the elevator up to the penthouse to talk with Alexandria. My phone rings, it's Susan. The twenty-four-hour security team I'm relocating to Santo Domingo is waiting to meet with me at the office before flying out. The crew finished the installation this morning, and I need to finalize my selections for the guards. Doesn't anyone take the holidays off anymore?

My relationships with Alexandria and my mother are equally strained, and all I wanted was a relaxing family Christmas. I thought Alexandria would love spending time with my family, and I was partially right. She and Tia Marie have been closed off in that sewing room for days. Alexandria seems to enjoy hanging out with her, but I wouldn't know because the woman has laid beside me every night and won't talk with me beyond a fucked up "yes" or a simple ass "no."

Like an idiot, my heart, my soul, and my body still want her. I lean forward using the wall for support, forcing myself to take a deep breath. Maybe it's some poor man's complex to want the thing you can't have, or some rich man's complex to think gifts, and patience, and fucking determination will get you the things that money can't buy. Because all I want is Alexandria's love.

And to think I considered extending an invitation to her folks. I knew Alexandria for four years, and we never spent the holidays with them as a couple. I quieted my fears about the Blackwells' dislike of me by focusing on the elephant in our relationship, finances. I was poor. She was not. I can understand how her grandfather would question that dynamic, it seemed like the apparent reason. The fact that I overcompensated by paying all the bills, and I loved Alexandria didn't mean a thing to them. But my race... Is my mother, right?

What would he say now? My mother's words cloud my thoughts, and this fucked up holiday. My parents, siblings, nieces, and nephews, and the woman I love are under one roof, yet this is not what I expected. Nothing is going as I hoped. *Nothing.*

Maybe Alexandria really is over our love, and what we had is a fond but distant memory.

Rage colors my sight red, and it's overshadowing the pure love I have for her. My mother's words make more sense than I want to admit. The door opens to my penthouse, and I glance inside.

I cross through my place. I've kept the team waiting

long enough. I quickly shower, and the moment I step out of the bathroom, I see Alexandria waiting for me.

I stop, and a place in me softens until I remember we haven't talked since she left me alone in the shower five days ago. The women in my life are conspiring against my sanity, except Tia Marie. She's the MVP this week. She took Alexandria to visit several quilt shops, and they've worked nonstop for a couple of days.

This is supposed to be a week of family, food, and fun. Instead, it's stressful and falls short of my vision. I need to call Liam and schedule flights to send everyone home. I want my life back. The voice in my head asks, *Without Alexandria?* I walk past her into the closet. She's on my heels.

"If you're waiting for an apology, I apologize," her voice holds a tremor.

"I don't want anything from you." I remove a dress shirt and reach for my favorite suit needing to feel some sort of control in my life. But I can't stop my eyes from caressing her. She's wearing her signature leggings, revealing every curve of her toned legs, and a *Kiss Me I'm Dominican* t-shirt that's covered in little bits of string. Her hair is still plaited from the other day, and there's a long white string hanging. I remove it.

"Thank you." I drop the thread in her hand, careful not to touch her.

Our eyes hold, and I realize there *is* something I want from her. I want to hear about her day. I want to go back to the Alexandria and Mateo we were at the engagement party. But that's not possible.

"We're here on a transactional basis. You helped get my parents here, and now I'll help assist with Platinum Prestige."

Her head jerks back as if she were slapped, and the faint glimmer of light fades from her eyes. I step around her to find a tie because I'm done trying.

I'm done extending myself for Alexandria. I'm done begging her to talk. I'm done asking her to see things from a different perspective.

I've tried to talk to her for days. My penthouse is big enough for us to coexist without disrupting each other.

Had I not witnessed the exchanges between Alexandria and my mother, I would have thought this holiday gathering is precisely as I've always dreamed. The family has shared every meal. She's smiled and kept up her end of the agreement.

"You can accompany me to the office. I'll be ready to leave in twenty minutes." I rake my eyes over her one last time wanting to hold her. I leave the closet.

I get dressed and wait in the car for thirty minutes. I dreamed of introducing her to my mother and to watch them merely coexist leaves me with more questions than answers. Alexandria is driving me insane. My body is not my own, my mind is not my own, and she's not mine either.

Alexandria hasn't come out, and I'm not going back

inside. I stare at my phone, debating whether to call her. There's a silent war being waged, and I hate losing.

Why fight the evitable? She doesn't want to be here, she doesn't feel comfortable here, and she obviously doesn't want me. I might as well stop torturing us both.

"Take me to the office."

CHAPTER 11

I stand at the window, watching the car leave, and I return to the closet. Tia Marie and Mateo's nieces and nephews are the only salvageable parts of this trip. I remove my phone and start calling the guys one by one. Then we managed to gather on a group call.

"Merry Christmas!!!"

I swipe at the tears, and a dull ache fills my body. I miss my guys. I miss my life in Austin. I'm not sure I can complete this assignment. Living through six months with Mateo isn't possible, not like this. They wait quietly as I try to wrangle my tears.

"Do we need to kick his ass?" Charlee jokes, and I can't laugh.

"Why'd I do this?" I hold the air in my chest. I hiccup and exhale. My body shaking violently, I hug my knees to my chest. "And his mother hates me."

"Hate is a strong word, honey." Harper's level tone doesn't work.

"Hate...hate...*hate*..." I grind the words out. I feel it every time she looks at me.

"Come home," Hunter demands.

"Liam..." Harper calls out, disappearing from her screen.

"I'm not quitting. I told him I'd stay through Christmas. But I decided I won't stay for the mentorship." I can't look at them because it's not all Mateo's fault.

The chatter of them talking over each other blurs the actual words. Don't worry about it. You'll be okay. Keep your head up. We'll work it out. And I miss the rest of the conversation because I'm caught in my own trap. I wanted to push him away, and I did, except this time, I pushed him too far.

"Fuck him." Charlee's tone cuts through the line.

"Dayum, who pied in your cereal and told you it was milk?" Payton chimes in, and we all freeze, staring at each other. I laugh for the first time in days. I fall back on his expensive plush carpet, in his big ass closet.

"You need to stop hanging around those bikers." I manage to say around my aching side. Payton is engaged to the president of a motorcycle club, and they're turning our pamper princess into a polished gem with a potty mouth.

"Not a chance. Cade has some single friends."

I glance down at my boulder. Mateo picked a

beautiful ring. It's like he embedded a source of light in the heart of it, making the diamond shine even in the dark.

"How can I salvage this situation?" I ask, glancing up at my guys.

"Start by telling us what happened." Ryann states.

I tell them about the shower and his family's arrival. Then I tell them about his mother's attitude.

"Talk to her. Woman to woman." Hunter concludes. "You both love the same man. You're probably more alike than not."

"What would I do without y'all?" I'm not sold on talking with Gloria, but I'll try. I notice the time. "I have to run. The Christmas party is starting in ten minutes."

"The plane will be on standby. Call us tonight." Harper adds.

"I will. Love you!"

I disconnect the line feeling better than before. I wash my face and change into a fresh shirt with no thread clinging to it. I finally finished repairing Mateo's quilt today. We visited a few shops, and I bought some New York inspired fabrics to patch up the holes. Then I used the leftovers to add a new scrappy binding with a mixture of Texas, New York, and Christmas designs.

I ride the elevator down to the main floor. The elevator opens, and everything is covered in white decorations. All except the adults in ugly sweaters.

"Hey, sobrina." Tia Marie walks over with a glass of wine. "Where's your sweater?"

"I don't have one." I'm floored by the transformation. "The food smells amazing."

"We're eating early. I'm too old to wait up until midnight." She laughs at her own joke. "Recheck the closet. Hurry, we'll wait for you."

"You guys can start." I turn to the elevator.

"Mateo will not have that. Go change." Tia Marie flicks a hand in my direction, and I return to the elevator.

I ride back up to the penthouse and return to the closet. There are several bags with my name on it. How had I missed them? Inside are wrapped gifts with names on the tags for the kids, lovingly signed *Love Uncle Mateo and Alex*. I've pissed him off, yet he's still looking out for me.

My throat thickens with emotion. These are our gifts for the exchange. I inspect the other bag and find the white elephant gifts. I pull out my phone to text Mateo and decide to call him *after* I call Susan.

"Thank you!" I say the moment she answers the line.

"You're welcome. Does the sweater fit?"

I put the phone on speaker and slip it on. "Yes, and I think I'll win the prize for the best ugly sweater." I laugh, looking in the mirror. "This is awful."

Susan laughs, "You better split the prize with me."

"Split what?"

"The hundred dollars," she squeals.

"Deal." I didn't know about the prize, but I'm down. We disconnect, and I call Mateo. He doesn't answer. I send a text message with a picture of me in the sweater, *Thank you!*

Seconds later, he responds, *You're welcome. I'll see you after my meeting. Have fun!*

I return downstairs.

The partying begins, and I forget I'm upset. There's something about Christmas. The lights, food, and family. They pull out board games, and I'm pulled into the fold. No one allows me to remain a bystander.

We laugh and get to know each other. Once we disperse, I head toward Gloria, thankful she meets me in the middle. She sits on the couch, patting the cushion beside her, and I sit.

Tia Marie throws up a thumb, and I smile. The others head to the kitchen to refill their drinks. I take a deep breath, ready to grovel if necessary. Then Gloria stops me.

"To the world, Mateo is this big, powerful businessman. To me, he's my firstborn and my baby. I'm sorry for the way I've behaved but not for looking out for my son. I've managed to ruin my son's Christmas, and I'm hoping you'll help me turn this thing around. Can we agree to try again?" Instead of extending a hand like before she opens her arms.

"I'd love to." I accept her apology and hug.

She holds me tight, and I hold her tighter. The

moment we pull back, I feel Mateo's presence behind me. I turn around, and we're wearing matching ugly sweaters.

"I'll leave you two alone." She pats my knee. She stops whispering in his ear before kissing him on the cheek.

"Thank you, Gloria."

"Call me, Mamá, mi hija." Hearing her call me daughter has me emotional.

Mateo opens his arms, and I find myself smothered in his embrace. "Are you okay?"

"I am now." I exhale.

I glance up, searching for the anger I've seen in the eyes all week. But up close, his anger looks more like what I'm feeling inside, disappointment.

"Can we talk later?" I ask.

"I'd like that."

"It's time for the gift exchange." Someone calls out, and we head into the family room.

We party until three in the morning. The kids open gifts and slowly start dropping one by one. Mateo and I say our goodnights and head up to his place. The elevator opens, and I'm on the couch before the door closes.

"I have a gift for you."

CHAPTER 12

*A*lexandria sits up alert. "I thought we don't exchange gifts until tomorrow."

"I want to give you this now." I pass her the envelope.

She slips her fingers underneath the fold and stops. The contents may change us forever. But I think it's the missing piece. The piece she's longed for from the moment I met her and I'm hoping by giving her him that she'll let me in.

I know my mother will come around, *but will Alexandria give us a second chance?*

She stares at the envelope, and I stare are her. I flex my antsy fingers, wanting to touch her. Then she sits it on the table, reaching for the hem of her sweater. I lose sight of her eyes for a moment as she slowly removes her clothes. Each garment lands on the floor, and she sits back waiting. Not saying a word.

I reach for my sweater and add it to hers. The items fall to the floor until we're naked. Eyes roaming.

"This is how I feel when I'm with you. Naked. Exposed. Vulnerable. Until tonight I saw it as a bad thing." Her knees curl up to her chest, and she releases them as if catching herself. "I don't want to pretend that I don't love you. Or that I don't miss you when you're gone. Or that seeing you and not being with you isn't the closest I've been to death."

I gather her head in my hands, and our mouths collide. I'm kissing her for the first time in almost a week, and I know how she feels.

I pull back, looking into her eyes. "I love you too."

MATEO LOWERS me to the bed, and his lips start at my toes. The kisses begin with a brush on my ankle cradled in his hand. His tongue blazes a trail up my calf until his lips kiss mine. I squirm under the power of his tongue. I can't hear the words over the adrenaline and untamed desire overtaking my body. He teases my clit, unlocking my thighs from around his neck.

My fingers run through his hair as he continues his journey, swirling his tongue in my bellybutton, nibbling on my nipples. He wraps my legs around his waist, and his thick cock brushes my waiting wetness, and he stops.

Tonight, for the first time in my entire life, I felt at home. And it was a feeling I longed for when I purchased my home and built my career and tirelessly pursued peace with every ounce of my will and power and independence. It was fleeting, never staying long, always close, but I could never convince it to stay. Then tonight, it came as I sat on the floor beside a white Christmas tree, in an ugly sweater wrapped in Mateo's arms.

I boldly brush my body against his. He sits back, staring down at me. His large hands spread my legs like wings, massaging my inner thighs. His finger swipes down my moist pussy, and I cry out.

"More of your foreplay, *mi querida*?" His eyes burn with hunger, and I want it all.

"No, love. Make love to me."

The need in his eye transforms into a ball of flames. He grabs the protection out of the side drawer, rolling it down his thick shaft and positions himself at my door. The rub of his head against my throbbing heat makes my hips move, I need him inside me, and I tell him.

"I told you, you'd want this. Didn't I?" A sinister smile spreads across his face matching the challenge in his eyes.

"Yes…" My pussy flickers. I'm done with this conversation.

"I want to hear you beg," he growls.

"After you." I push him back and take him in my mouth.

"Oh…fuck!"

I would laugh, but my mouth is busy. I take him until he fills the walls of my mouth. I work him until he can't utter another cocky word.

I want him to feel the earth move. I want to him to feel the insanity of us. I want to relieve the ache of the pain I caused him. I want to fill him with pleasure and joy, and wholeness. I want him to love me.

Walking around mad at the world taught me a lot about myself. What if this is my second chance? What if I can be wholly accepted and completely loved? The veins of his cock quiver against my tongue. He growls, trying to slip away, but I grip the base, massaging his balls in my hands, still taking all of him.

"My turn."

I'm on my back so fast a laugh escapes. His face is between my thighs, tongue diving deep. My legs start shaking, and the pleasure of release is drawing closer.

"Aaahhhh…."

"Beg…" He demands. "Now…*mi alma.*"

I buck off the bed, but my hips are locked in his strong embrace. "Matty…"

He sits back, and it all stops. He grips the shift of his cock, teasing my pulsing heat.

"This is torture."

"No, it's foreplay." He crawls up my body, his hot skin blazing mine until his mouth hovers over mine. I kiss him tasting myself. I wiggle my hands between us, trying to slip his cock inside, but he stops me. "Say please, *mi alma.*"

"Please…" If I'm his soul, he's mine. And I knew it from the moment we met.

He slides in, and my eyes fill with tears. He strokes the fire he started, we're both groaning, lost in the moment. Words of love are whispered over my skin. I bite, scratch, and brand his body as mine until he races us to our death.

"Fuck…." He growls, falling beside me. My eyes dip closed. "Alexandria, you're mine. Here or Texas, I don't care. But we do it together."

"I know…"

CHAPTER 13

*A*lexandria clenches the sheet to her chest. The tension etched across her beautiful face threatens to scrub this exhilarating moment from my mind. We broke her one rule. Not deliberately, but we killed it. I made love to her all night, and we can't take it back.

"Merry Christmas, mi amour," I whisper. Her head turns, her black waves spill across my sheets. She holds the sheet tighter, her eyes search mine.

I could have denied her request, but the moment her sweet lips locked around my cock compulsion took over. She didn't beg or plead the way I envisioned. But her soft request erased the fight in me.

"Merry Christmas, Mateo." The words are strained.

I can apologize and say I never intended for this to happen, but it would be a blatant lie. I was made to make love to her. So, instead of lying to her, I'll feed her and show her my love.

"How about we have breakfast tacos?"

She shakes her head, and I see the softest smile. "You can't cook, and Mama shouldn't be asked to cook. It's Christmas."

"I got the keys to the city. I can find some Tex-Mex tacos even on Christmas Day." I wait and feel compelled to add. "We'll be okay, love."

Her eyes fill with tears. "Promesa?"

I cover her body with mine. "What is it?"

"Promise me, Mateo."

We're back here. What did I expect? That she'd be thrilled to be back in my life. That I'd make love to her, and she'd see the error in her thinking. That she'd see we belong together. *No existe gran talento sin gran voluntad.*

I gather her face in my hands. My will and my love will overpower her doubts. "I promise. Now tell me you'll stay." I kiss her. Praying, I quiet the fears in her, and she'll trust that our love can banish anything trying to keep us apart.

"I'll stay."

I SNUGGLE BACK into my ugly sweater and head to the main floor in search of coffee. Mateo has a full kitchen in his penthouse with no food. But I know Gloria won't fail me. She usually has the first pot of coffee brewing by five.

I head to the elevator and see the envelope from last night. I grab it. It feels soft and flexible, like a letter. I'll read it while I drink my coffee.

I follow the aroma. "I think I love you."

Gloria laughs. "Merry Christmas."

"Merry Christmas to you too." I pull down a mug and pour a cup. I lean against the counter for my first sip. I smile as the liquid coats my insides.

"Thank you." Gloria lowers her mug to the island.

"For what?"

"Mateo had a smile this big." Her arms open, and we chuckle.

"We're heading in the right direction." I exhale taking another drink of my coffee. We're not perfect, but we're certainly better.

"And…I realize my attitude had more to do with your grandfather. I'm so sorry for taking it out on you."

The coffee rolls down the wrong pipe, and I choke. "My grandfather?"

My ears pop in terror at the mention of my grandfather. I look around out of instinct and back at her.

"I'll never forgive him for the way he ran my son off." She pats my back, and I'm trying to figure out what she's talking about. "To offer to pay him off, like his some...some *azarar*." Her mouth sets in a tight grimace.

"...*azarar*?" She's made it a point to speak in English all week. I speak Spanish, but I'm not familiar with the word.

"Who are you speaking of sister?" Tia Marie walks in the kitchen and sits beside Gloria.

"Mr. Blackwell."

I don't miss the discreet shake Tia Marie gives Gloria. I swallow, trying to stop the sinking feeling in my chest.

"What does my grandfather have to do with Mateo?" I face Tia Marie, but she's avoiding my questioning eyes. "What does it mean?"

"Like...bad luck, as in not good for you."

I gaze off piecing it together. Ran Mateo off... Offered to pay... "My grandfather paid him to leave." My world is spinning and riddled with questions.

Does my mother know? When did this happen? Why didn't anyone tell me? Darkness is closing in, and I shouldn't be surprised. I knew my grandfather had it in him. But I'm not someone he can control.

My phone chimes. I glance at the screen, *We're here*.

The cavalry. What are they doing here? I unlock my phone to respond and realize I forgot to call them last night. Harper and Liam sent a plane for me.

I hop off the stool, "Huh...I need to make a quick run."

Tia Marie appears in front of me. "Shouldn't you wait for Mateo?"

I run off, deciding not to wait for the elevator. I take the stairs two at a time until I reach Mateo's place.

Where? I respond, throwing my clothes in a bag.

Four Seasons.

CHAPTER 14

*T*ia Marie wouldn't allow me to take a cab. So, I accepted her offer to use her driver, and after I tip him, I enter the hotel.

"Ho...ho...ho...."

The Santa standing in the lobby is shady AF as I do the walk of shame. A week ago, I arrived in this hotel in a ten-thousand-dollar gown, dripping in diamonds. Today, I'm walking through the lobby with an ugly sweater, leggings, with sandals and socks.

I accepted this assignment with one caveat: Don't land in Mateo's bed. But oh no, I had to taunt the man and now the jokes on me.

I knock on the suite door. It swings open, and there's a collective gasp.

"Ahhh...shyte. He had you speaking in tongues, didn't he?" Charlee is throwing it back, and I'm confused.

"Huh..." Harper runs a hand over the top of her

perfectly coifed hair, in a smoothing motion. I shrug it off, not understanding since her hair is in cornrows.

"Had you calling him Papi?" Charlee says with a fake accent.

I walk into the room, dropping my bag on the floor. I slump into the chair folding over. "My grandfather paid him to leave."

"Ricco Suave?

"What are you talking about, Charlee?" I yell and sit up to see her cockeyed smile. The others are fighting to hold back laughter. "What's so damn funny? My life is crumbling around me and—"

Harper passes me a mirror.

"I look like a madwoman." Kill me. Right now. *Please*. "I walked across that lobby with that fucking Santa calling me a ho."

Tears are running down Chase's face. Ryann's shaking like she's about to have a seizure.

Jordan has the decency to look me in the eye, coughing in her hand. "But your sweater is… huh…festive."

The ripple of snickers starts, and I hate them, each and every one. Harper snorts, gasping for air with a tight hold on her baby bump.

"I can't stand y'all heifas," I whine, and the dam breaks wide open.

The roar of their laughter is deafening. They're falling over each other. Hooting and hollering. It's a scene out of the funniest movie and my worst nightmare.

"That must have been one hell of a night. Santa tore that stuff up." Charlee howls like she's about to die.

And I sit in amazement. I shake my head, looking in the mirror again. The shit is funny. My hair is packed on my head because I didn't wear a bonnet last night. Yesterday's makeup is smeared across my face, and I'm wearing a sweater with flashing Christmas lights.

I hear a knock at the door. I walk over to get it since none of them can compose themselves.

"Y'all better not ask me for nothing when we get back to Austin." I open the door and freeze.

"Alexandria."

"TIA MARIE."

I could hear their laughter the moment I walked out of the elevator. Now, nine sets of eyes are glued on us.

"We need to talk." She opens her mouth to refuse. "Now, we can do it in front of your friends, in the lobby, or on the *fucking* moon. But we're going to talk this out."

The laughter dies as the women right themselves and walk over. I take a moment to look at them as they stand behind Alexandria. Nine women sporting designer clothing and their baby bumps. They traveled from Austin to support her, and my wall of rage crumbles.

"They can do or say what they want, but I'm not leaving. Because you and I promised."

An eerie slice falls over the room. I'm standing in the doorway, not entirely inside but not fully out. The women surround Alexandria, one holding her hand, another with an arm wrapped around her waist.

"I'll listen."

I'm not sure who says it because my eyes are on Alexandria. I glance over and receive a quick wave from a lady over Alexandria's shoulder.

"I almost lost Zach due to a misunderstanding. I've always vowed to hear the full story before deciding." She glances over at the others.

I plead with Alexandria from my heart to hers and wait until I see a slight nod. "Your grandfather came to our place one day and offered me five thousand dollars."

There's a collective gasp, and Alexandria's eyes turn ice cold. "Did you take it?"

"No." I step inside until I clear the doorway. I reach for her.

"They why did you leave?" The words rip from her soul, and I want to hold her.

"Because I didn't want you to have to choose between them and me. They're your family."

"You were my family." She shouts and struggles to remain composed.

"Correction. I *am* your family." Her fearless warriors step back, and I take another step. "I regret not coming to you, but I couldn't ask you to walk away knowing I had nothing to give you."

"All I ever needed was you."

"Well, you got me, baby."

"That's that Rico Suave *shyte*."

"Charlee." They chide in unison.

"What? Don't act like I'm the only one that noticed."

Alexandria rolls her eyes, and she steps into my arms. A chorus of aahhhhs surrounds us. These women are fascinating. I brush my lips across hers, and I'm rewarded with a kiss.

I pull back. "Would you ladies like to join us for brunch?"

"No, thank you. We have to get back. Are you staying Alexandria?"

I wrap an arm around her waiting for her answer. "Yes, I'll call you guys later."

"Then, it's time to roll out."

The ladies start gathering their bags, and I turn to Alexandria, "Love...your hair."

"I know," she groans.

They laugh all the way to the lobby, and Alexandria says her goodbyes. The moment the SUV is out of sight, she turns to me. "I'm ready to go home."

I ENTER THE HOUSE, and everyone's waiting for me.

Gloria looks relieved, and Tia Marie holds me close to her chest.

"Welcome home," Tia Marie shouts.

"I know you sent him."

"She didn't have to send me, I wouldn't let you get away twice. Once almost killed me." I kiss him with all the love I have in my heart. "I'll be right back."

"Oh no, you don't!" Gloria yells.

"I'm just going to quilt room to get Mateo's gift."

I run up the stairs and return with a box. Mateo, a man with everything, stares at the box with tears in his eyes. "Thank you, *mi alma*."

"You don't even know what it is. Open it." I push the box closer.

Mateo peels away the metallic white wrapping paper and opens the cardboard box. He knows what it is. He leans over the table, and his mouth covers mine. "Thank you."

"Pull it out."

He removes the quilt and opens it wide. Gloria and Tia Marie hold each side. Even his father gasps. I repaired his old seams and patched up the holes. I made it bigger by adding pictures from the last week. There's one with him and his parents, him and his siblings, him and Tia Marie, and us. I even added a picture of the kids. The gratitude in his eyes melts away any lingering doubts.

"Now open yours." I almost forgot about the envelope. I return to my bag and pull it out. I glance around, smiling as everyone waits. I remove the letter. My eyes scan across the words. It's the address and number for Antonio Martinez in Guadalajara. I look up at Mateo with the paper crumbled in my sweaty hands.

"You found my father." I'm too stunned to cry.

He nods. "We can visit him if you like."

There's no other man for me. I'll have to deal with my mother and grandfather. But I'm not giving Mateo up again, and I'm ready to learn more about the other part of me.

"I would." I fly into his arms. He kisses me, and it eases all the turmoil I feel down in my soul.

"Can we eat? I'm starving." His father calls out, and the family heads into the kitchen.

Mateo leads me by the hand, and I can't contain the smile on my face or the joy in my heart.

Hours later, we head to bed after the kids open the rest of their gifts. Mateo is floating around the place after his parents decided to stay until the new year, and I don't blame him. The moment the door closes, he starts removing my clothes until I'm naked in my engagement ring. He drops to one knee.

"Will you marry me?"

"Yes!"

I undress him taking my sweet time, running my hands all over his body when the realization that he's all mine settles over me. I kiss across his chest, pushing back to the bed. I climb on top of him.

I stare into his eyes. "I love you. I never stopped loving you."

"I love you too."

I lower until he fills me. We make love until the new day greets us. He kisses me, and I watch sleep take him.

I came to New York for an assignment, scared to face Mateo and our past. I don't know what the future holds, but if it's more of him, I'm ready and willing. This truly is a Merry Christmas.

I'll have to thank Jordan, her Christmas wish worked. And not only did I get my man, but I got a new family too. Not bad for a...*ho...ho...ho*.

EPILOGUE

Six months later...

The doors of the conference room open, and a hush falls over the room. The GIB enters, and I lean forward to watch my woman lead the guys inside.

Alexandria moved to New York and never left. My parents stayed around, and when my mother heard Alexandria was pregnant, I finally convinced them to make New York our home as a family. My mansion is finally full of my family, and my woman is full with our child.

There's only one more thing to cross off my list. I stand motioning to the vacant chairs. "Guys. Welcome."

I smile over at Susan, and she shakes her head abreast of my plans. But Alexandria will have us old and grey before she decides on every detail of the wedding. Her relationship with her father is growing every day. Her mother and stepfather plan to spend time with us this summer. Her grandfather threatened to disown her, but when Alexandria stood up to him and tossed her bank statement on the desk, he promptly shut up. So, their relationship is strained but not broken.

Now is the time to make my fake fiancé my real wife.

"Thank you all for joining us. Alexandria and I have structured a plan to help you move into the international market. But I have also created a plan that will allow you to onboard international clients while limiting your exposure and expenses."

"I'm listening," the seductive spread of her smile makes me rock hard.

"I can help you, Alexandria. But...I have a request." Sitting at the head of the boardroom table is a turn on for her, I'm sure we conceived our son in this very room.

"Okay. And that is?"

The love I see in her eyes makes me feel like the richest man in the world. "Marry me? Today."

"Matty..."

There's a collective gasp in the room, and I take advantage of their shock. "I don't want a perfect wedding. I only need you to say two words, I do."

"But..."

"Everyone's here and waiting."

"Everyone? Here?" She glances around as if expecting them to enter the conference room.

I nod, "They are patiently waiting at the Four Seasons. Your parents. Your father. Your grandfather. Your guys…"

"You," she whispers, and her eyes beam with love.

"Do you require anything else, *mi alma*?"

"No, all I ever needed was you. I accept."

I circle the table to kiss my lady. Charlee stands up, clapping with the guys. She opens her mouth to speak, and Alexandria stops. "Charlee Raine, I swear if you say one word about freaky *shyte* I'm might scream."

"Says the woman ready to get it on on the table. I can see it in your eyes. He started talking in Spanish, and you started drooling."

I shake my head. This is our life. Now to marry my lady before she realizes we didn't discuss her international expansion. I guide her to the door, "You ready to become Mrs. Rodriquez?"

She pulls back and whispers, "How long have you been planning this? Did Susan help? How much did you spend?"

I make the motion of zipping my mouth. "I'm about to lavish you with everything my money can buy." I pull up behind her brushing my aroused state against her full bottom. "I got the DJ from the engagement party."

Alexandria's head snaps in my direction. "Slicker than oil, but I love you."

"I need you to show me how much on the dance floor." Her head falls back as laughter spills over. We walk up to the waiting car, and I glance up at the sky for the briefest moment and whisper, *Thank you* for our second chance. I climb in beside Alexandria, ready for the first day of our forever.

~

THANK you for reading **LAVIS LOVE**. Alexandria and Mateo found their happily ever after. Please leave a review. Keep reading and meet Chase and Jameson in *Total Love*. The FINAL book in the Blazin' Love Series.

It's New Year's Eve.

Business is insane, and my life is unrecognizable, thanks to the bundle of joy I carried home from my last trip to Las Vegas. But exceeding a billion dollars is worth celebrating until I see my son's father.

I'm Chase Elliott. The GIB boarded a private flight to the City of Second Chances to celebrate our 10th Anniversary. A weekend is all I need to pop in and out of his city until Jameson enters the club.

The man who devoured my body and changed my life. The man who haunts my dreams, craving him, is etched in the fibers of my soul.

And I fold to my last mistake of the old year, and in the heat of passion, I reveal our son has his eyes. I slip into the New Year running home under a cloud of Jameson's threat—my hand or his son.

I'm prepared to fight the man who confiscated my heart. And as the truth comes to the light, I only hope lies don't tear down the house that love built.

One-click TOTAL LOVE now!

CHAPTER ONE

"*P*erfection." I purse my cherry red lips in the mirror ensuring my face is beat to capacity, and it is. I run a hand over my sleek ponytail, dropping it over my shoulder, ready to dance off this sour mood. I add an extra coat of lipstick. Red always makes me feel strong and in control.

"Well, pack your hottest two pieces. I plan to return looking like an Egyptian goddess." I add my two cents to the robust conversation on our three-way call.

I wink at myself picking up the phone while my besties Charlee and Harper gush over my recent invitation. Nobody, and I do mean *nobody* throws a better soiree than me. Theme, destination, transportation, no detail overlooked, because every element is significant. Every element is hand-selected to etch the experience in the minds of my guests forever.

Charlee and Harper talk back and forth as I walk to my closet discussing what they're packing. Who knew I'd need this trip? Not to celebrate Valentine's Day with Lewis, who's no longer my boyfriend but my *ex*-boyfriend, instead, I need this trip to take a break from Austin. I need time to scrub his lying, cheating, no good ass from my life. I need a change.

I turn my face from the screen, not wanting them to see how much his cheating effects me. But Lewis ain't worth a single tear. The dick pic he obviously sent me by accident marked the end of our on-again, off-again relationship. The message flashes before my eyes, *B, your lollipop misses you.*

I should have blocked him a long time ago. But I got comfortable. We travel in the same social circle. We shared some of the same interests. We had something once, but apparently that was a lie too. I mean, how special can I be if he's sending dick pics to women?

"So, you and Lewis don't have a hot date tonight?" Harper asks pulling me out of my unhealthy thoughts.

"Nah, he's doing him, and I'm doing me. Tonight's about us helping you find a man." I see the tears glistening in her eyes. "Harper, one day you'll find a man who appreciates you for the amazing woman you are. Then you'll be glad you kicked he who shall remain nameless' no good ass to the curb."

"*Under* the curb," Charlee snapped. Harper's tight smile isn't fooling me, as she brushes away a tear the moment it leaves her eye.

"No more tears Harper. Tonight, we're going to Brew & Boujee. Get ready to have some fun and have too many drinks!" I joke trying to cheer her up. I'm determined to sit through a million blind dates to see her smile.

Harper is a good one, she increases our average. She's the swan waiting to show her full potential, and that bastard will roast in hell. Guaranteed.

So, tonight is not about me or Lewis, tonight is for Harper. Lewis is a liar. I know it. He knows it. His deception came as no surprise. And now, I'm a walking, talking billboard used by old school R&B songs as evidence of how hard it is for a good woman to find a good man. Because that dog bit me in my ass *again*, so now the joke's on me for forgiving him *again*. Thanks to Lewis, love is not on my agenda.

"I want the drinks and the men." Charlee tipped a glass in our direction.

Sounds like I'm not the only one nursing a cracked heart or a bruised ego. I think it's more of the latter. I didn't love Lewis, maybe it was the prospect of love I loved. Harper raises an eyebrow in my direction but neither of us asks questions about Charlee's tipsy state, I guess we've learned to coexist in our own worlds. And I'm thankful. Most people would consider us shallow, or self-centered. I like that we support each other without being all up in each other's business, besides I'm not ready to share my blues either. Not until I can explain how I keep finding myself back here, with another no good, gorgeous, rich, shallow, douche of a man.

Charlee is entertaining us with another one of her hookups gone wrong. I climb the stairs in my closet and place my phone on the island. The first floor holds my everyday clothes, shoes, and accessories. The second floor is where I store my glam.

The far wall holds my evening gowns, cocktail dresses, and formal attire. The island is full of jewelry and all the knick-knacks that make dressing up elegant and fun. I scan the area in front of me, trying to decide where to start my search. I need an outfit to make a statement.

My girls are baddies, always dressed to impress. Plus there's a chance I'll see Lewis tonight. I push the clothes around searching for my best *f'him* outfit.

"I'm down for this trip. Anything to get away from my nagging parents," Charlee adds finally taking a breath. "That's the one Hunt."

I stop sliding the last hanger back. "Red on Valentine's Day is cliché and you know that's not my style."

"Yeah, maybe on someone else but not on you," Harper says.

I pull the dress down, turning the phone towards the ceiling to floor mirror. I inspect the tag. The crimson bodycon dress fit me like a glove in the swank Austin boutique. I shrug holding it against me. The spaghetti straps compliment my brown skin. The deep v-neck neckline means I have to go braless to pull it off. The knee length is the only tame feature. It's definitely a statement dress, leaving little to the imagination.

"Hunter."

"I'm in here Daddy," I call over my shoulder. "We'll talk at S&J," I tell Charlee and Harper.

"What time is the reservation?"

"Now for your late tail," Harper teases Charlee.

"Whatever! Perfection takes time ladies."

"The speed dating starts at seven. We need to get there early to get the best seats," I tell them. This argument is the center of their existence, Harper is always early, Charlee is always late.

"Which means, Charlee, sweetheart, if *you* want a man, *you* need to get there on time." I laugh glad to see Harper's spunk coming back.

"You know what Harper Anne," Charlee adds a country twang to her voice, "you can shove it where the sun don't—"

"Hunter, what is this?" I jump startled by my father at the top of the stairs. He is waving a sheet of paper in the air. I roll my eyes glancing back at my phone.

"All right later dudes. I'll see y'all in a few. Save me a seat."

We say our goodbyes and hang up. I drop to the couch beside the island facing him. The frown on my Daddy's face tells me he's gearing up for a lecture.

"Hey Daddy, how was your day?" My heart rate

spikes at seeing his handsome face twisted in disappointment. I paste a smile on my face aiming for my best sweet-as-pie grin to cancel out the scowl on his.

My parents joke that I'm their perfect creation. I have my mother's alluring eyes and pouty lips. But I'm my father's twin, from my brown skin to my taller than average height. I have his slightly wide nose and his smile. A smile I use like a Black AmEx to gain access to anywhere and anything. However, proves defective tonight.

"Hunter we need to talk, now. Meet me in my office."

This is bad. I don't mind pissing people off, but not Daddy. He holds the keys to this mansion, and quite honestly I care what he thinks even though he has a tendency to overreact.

"Can we talk later? The girls and I have reservations," I offer hoping to give him time to cool off, to rethink whatever is scattering around that head of his.

He lets out a heavy sigh. "Five minutes Hunt." Then he stalks off.

I grab my phone. What have I done to bring this on? I search my mind coming up empty-handed. Let me lay my clothes out and then go see what he wants.

I grab a pair of stilettos and toss them on the floor. I open a drawer finding earrings, a necklace, and I push around my rings looking for my favorite chunky ring for my middle finger. I lay them out on top of the island. That should cut down the time I need to get ready. I can't be late.

I leave my room walking through the house towards Daddy's office. Our house is quiet, as the staff moves around invisible. The only sound I hear is my shuffling slides. I lightly tap on his door.

"Have a seat." Daddy rubs the back of his neck, turning in his chair. He's in his high back leather chair behind a desk large enough to seat at least six people. He leans forward resting his hands on top. The pose would seem harmless if I didn't see steam rising from his ears.

"What is it, Daddy? You're scaring me."

"Hunter, I'm at my wits end with you." He runs a hand over his face, letting out a deep sigh. My father is the soft one of my parents. He doesn't raise his voice. He's reasonable. He's level headed. All I have to do is smile and apologize, and he'll hide my dead bodies from the world, even my mother.

"Whatever it is, I'm sorry Daddy." Blink. Blink. I add a good batting of my lashes for good measure.

"Baby, I don't believe you."

"What?" I hold my breath until my lungs burn, screaming for relief.

"Things have got to change around here." His hands steeple in front of him, and my heart drops. He lifts a sheet of paper tossing it in my direction. I pick it up from the desk, and immediately I hear the sounds of crashing metal against metal in my head, like a thousand car pileup.

"You approved the trip." *Sort of.* I can't whisper the truth that I had to top my last trip. The pressure of every event being compared to the last is real.

"Hunter Josephine Preston, where do you get off spending six figures on a vacation?"

Oh shit, this is serious. When Black parents use your first, middle, and last name, shit is about to hit the fan.

"Where are you going, to the moon first class?"

"No, I thought I'd take a little celebratory vacation with my friends." I scan the sheet of paper. The private jet, the yacht, the private resort, and the red ink circled around the grand total. I feel sweat gathering under my armpits. "I got a good deal."

I say the words as I put the receipt back on his desk. But they're a lie too. I didn't ask for the numbers. I said what I wanted and gave Daddy's credit card number.

"Hunter I bust my ass to give you this life. And you don't get it." His finger thrusts in my direction.

"I'll cancel it, Daddy. I just—"

"You just what Hunt? You have no respect for money. How do I know? *Because* you spend it like you earn it. Like it grows on trees. Like I don't get up every morning, get dressed, and carry my ass to the office and work."

I see that little vein in the middle of his forehead, and I pray the floor opens and takes me whole. But there is no love for me today. It's like the men in my life had a secret meeting, and I'm getting a two-for-one deal.

All jokes aside, I can't deny the power behind his words as they vibrate off the walls. This wasn't my intent yet I hear the pain in his tone, and it's shooting daggers through my heart better than cupid ever has. I glance down at my hands feeling two inches tall. I can't stand to see the disappointment in his eyes.

"Do you know that it takes most people years to earn this kind of money?" I glance up, and he's shaking the receipt around again. I canvas my mind for a logical reason. And I don't have one, except I did it because I could. Daddy always says yes. Except today.

I can't watch.

"Junior…"

I look up, maybe it's not so bad. I'm an only child. I was their last attempt at in vitro. I am their miracle baby.

My mother had such a hard time getting pregnant that she named me after my father because she knew they'd have no more kids. I'm it. And that's how a woman ends up with a man's name.

"Daddy, I'm truly sorry. I won't do it again."

"I know you won't." The finality in his voice makes the hairs on my neck stand at attention. "Go get my card and your cellphone."

For the next thirty minutes, my father scrubs my phone and payment systems of his credit card information. I wish he'd yell and scream. Instead, his silence is killing me.

"But Daddy…" is all I can say.

"One day you'll thank me for this."

I can't see it. "Are you cutting me off?"

"No, Hunter I'm teaching you how to grow up."

HUNTER AND BEN are about to set your Kindle on fire. (Don't say I didn't warn you.) You can read PLATINUM LOVE now and start at the beginning with the guys of Platinum Prestige.

AUTHOR'S NOTE

I said YES to a holiday romance writing project in 2019.

Ten authors. Ten holidays. Ten steamy romances. And we've all said yes to taking this journey together.

My ten stories are novella length. I think they're great for an evening of reading with your favorite glass of wine or tea. :) And I had the group of guys to make this series happen.

Then struts in Hunter and her squad, her guys. They came to me years ago. I love a good millionaire or billionaire romance like the next woman. But a few of my readers emailed me asking about a female millionaire. I thought why settle for one if I can write ten. **insert evil laugh**

I hope you enjoyed book one with Alexandria and Mateo. Will you join me for the rest of the year as they build Platinum Prestige—one fly millionaire woman and hot guy at a time?

Don't miss a single release. Join my newsletter at **http://www.janesedixon.com/subscribe** to get updates and reader specials FIRST.

In closing, please leave a review. It helps others find my work and it keeps the lights on, if you know what I mean. ;)

I'll "see" you all soon.

Happy Reading,
Ja'Nese Dixon
www.janesedixon.com

P.S. Again, there are more Steamy Sensations Holiday Love stories available now. See them all on my website: http://www.janesedixon.com/steamy-sensations.

LEAVE A REVIEW

Did you enjoy *Select Love*?

Please leave a book review **HERE**. Reviews are extremely important and it helps me continue sharing my books with fellow readers.

SIGN UP!

Be the FIRST to know!

Consider joining my newsletter? http://www.janesedixon.com/subscribe Be the first to know about releases and specials. You can unsubscribe anytime.

BOOK 1

It's Valentine's Day.

I run to my favorite bar determined to figure out how I managed to lose my man and my inheritance in one night. The man is replaceable, but my monthly stipend is not.

I'm Hunter Preston. My friends call me Jo and I'm the only child to a media mogul. I was traveling the world, living my best life, until Daddy dropped a million-dollar bomb, annihilating my boujee world.

Double or nothing.

He gave me thirty days to pitch a million dollar business concept, or I can say goodbye to my trust fund.

So, here I am with my girls, trying to get more than selfie advice, when Ben, the sexy bartender— who either abhors me or he's immune to my flirting

—offers to help write the business plan under one condition. He wants $50,000.

$50k to get $1 mil sounds reasonable until I remember how hot he is and how off-limits he is and how he wants nothing to do with a woman like me.

I'm screwed, pass me another drink.

Get Your Copy on Amazon
or Read in Kindle Unlimited!

Read an excerpt on www.janesedixon.com.

BOOK 2

It's St. Patrick's Day.

The day is really not important, at least that's what I thought. I dress to impress, ready to secure my first contract as a partner with Platinum Prestige.

Simple, right? No, I wish.

I'm Harper Price. I've joined my best friends in starting an elite concierge service and I'm up. My sole task is to lease an airplane from Liam.

I walk in, he proposes, I walk out.

Apparently, his billionaire have gone to his head and now the sexy, arrogant menace won't leave me alone. His head is hard as a brick. (Take that any way you want.) And he refuses to accept "no" in any language. But I'm done with love.

No more.

Nada.

No mas.

Yet secretly, I'm scribbling my first name with his last name. Then he whispers, "Live a little Harper." And his money green eyes shine like dollars signs as he throws an unexpected curve ball. He'll grant three wishes, when…not if…I say yes.

Does having the most eligible rich bachelor begging to put a ring on it make me lucky? Hell no!

Not when my heart is screaming leap, my head is screaming caution, and my panties are.…

Oh hell, this is a f'in plane crash waiting to happen.

What is a woman to do?

**Get Your Copy on Amazon
or Read in Kindle Unlimited!**

Read an excerpt on www.janesedixon.com.

BOOK 10

He lied to get laid... I lie to hide our truth...

It's New Year's Eve.

Business is insane, and my life is unrecognizable, thanks to the bundle of joy I carried home from my last trip to Las Vegas. But exceeding a billion dollars is worth celebrating until I see my son's father.

I'm Chase Elliott. The GIB boarded a private flight to the City of Second Chances to celebrate our 10th Anniversary. A weekend is all I need to pop in and out of his city until Jameson enters the club.

The man who devoured my body and changed my life. The man who haunts my dreams, craving him, is etched in the fibers of my soul.

And I fold to my last mistake of the old year, and in the heat of passion, I reveal our son has his eyes. I slip into the New Year running home under a cloud of Jameson's threat—my hand or his son.

I'm prepared to fight the man who confiscated my heart. And as the truth comes to the light, I only hope lies don't tear down the house that love built.

**Get Your Copy on Amazon
or Read in Kindle Unlimited!**

Read an excerpt on www.janesedixon.com.

Millions of adoring fans dream of having one night with him, but only she has access to his heart.

Born with three commas in his bank account and melodies in his veins, Marques Carter is the rising prince of R&B. But not even his family name can guarantees success.

Brione Allen is a smart woman that made a dumb decision: trusting the wrong man. He blackmailed her family and now she's bound by a debt they knew she couldn't pay.

A chance meeting at his concert leads to an encrypted proposal: One week, one hundred thousand dollars, one incriminating secret. But when extortion and family ties expose them to the worst of the limelight, which secrets will they keep...and which will threaten their small light of hope?

**Get Your Copy on Amazon
or Read in Kindle Unlimited!**

CHAPTER 1

The same time every week for three years and the call got no easier. Brione Allen sat on the couch and blew out a deep breath. Dial the number. Ask for Kayla. But the knot in her stomach told the utter truth. Nothing about this was easy for her.

She tapped the numbers by memory, adding it to her favorites was something she couldn't stomach, not after all they'd done to her.

"Hello."

"Good evening Mrs. Bradley is Kayla around?" She stopped asking to speak with her hoping to gain a sense of control in the situation, but they held her captive with a vice grip on her heart.

"Hello to you too Brione." Her dusty voice held an air of censorship. "I'll call for her."

Kayla had a nanny, private school, and just about everything a little girl could want.

"Brione." She cringed at hearing his voice.

"Stewart, I was holding for Kayla."

"She'll have to call you back."

"But today is my—"

"Talk to you later."

The line disconnected and Brione screamed. No one heard her, and no one cared. Alone in her fancy plush prison, she'd gladly trade for their freedom.

She fell back on the couch and stared at the ceiling fan and her cellphone rang. She popped up anticipating the sweet sound of Kayla's voice. But the screen displayed another welcomed caller.

"Eliana Marshall. To what do I owe this honor?" Laughter flowed through the phone, Eliana was the only person she let close. The only person she trusted. The only person who knew the truth.

"Let's see...I'm your best friend. So I need no reason to call other than to hear your wonderful voice." Brione smiled. "Second, I'm flying into town, and I refuse any excuse you make for not seeing me."

Brione gripped the phone to her ear as she toyed with the hem of her blouse. She'd rushed home from work for nothing.

"I apologized a million times. But you plan to milk it dry," she joked pulling her stocking covered feet beneath her body and relaxed.

"I plan to milk it until it turns to powder if that will

get your butt out of that condo. I will *not* take no for an answer."

"Milk it dry *and* add in a level of guilt to the recipe."

"You got it." They laughed. "How are you?"

"I've been better." Brione looked around the room, furnished with the finest, reeking of their wealth. "You're heading here for the weekend?"

"No, I'm heading back indefinitely. Bruce and his wife are expecting twins, and they're keeping a close watch on her. We're planning to hang out in Houston until the babies arrive. Her doctor and family are all there. So, it could be a couple of months or longer."

"Yay!" Brione sat up, excited. "It will be nice to have you in town for a while."

"Just know I plan to pop up on your doorstep and drag you to a party or two while I'm there." Brione shook her head knowing they would have a battle ahead.

"How are you enjoying your job?"

Brione listened as Eliana shared her love of working for Bruce Daniels. She bounced around from Atlanta to Houston and back as his assistant.

"I can't believe the luck I've had with getting this job. It is stressful but fun. I'll be assisting Marques for a while too."

"Who is that?" The name sounded familiar, in a fuzzy, vague way.

"What rock do you live under?"

"The law school rock." She snickered. "I don't have

time for anything but class and studying. Well, that and my side gig."

"Side gig?"

"Eliana, who is Marques?"

"Oh, yeah. How do you *not* know who he is?" Her amazement was evident by the squeak in her voice. "He's a caramel dipped...tall, muscled...*god* in living color."

Brione lifted a brow at Eliana's description. "All that?"

"Yes, he's the epitome of sexy. Too bad he's my boss." She let out a sigh. "Anyway, he's an R&B singer from Atlanta. I guess you wouldn't know him since he's more underground." She was all business. "He is the flagship artist of Rockstar Entertainment. We're preparing to release an EP then his debut album."

Brione tried to picture this caramel sexy god. Her failed attempt morphed into her last dalliance that turned her life upside down, inside out, and left Brione estranged from her family.

"That sounds like a lot of work." Brione didn't listen to the radio and rarely watched TV. Her sights were set on securing an associate's position with a major law firm. Fun took a backseat.

"It is, which is part of the reason for my call." Eliana said.

"Oh, it wasn't just to hear my wonderful voice?"

"Of course."

"Yeah, yeah, yeah. Spill it, Honey." Brione walked to

the kitchen and opened the freezer, pushing around the contents until she found the frozen lasagna.

"Do you still help with events?"

"Yes, what's up?" She peeled back the corner of the lid and popped the plastic bowl into the microwave. Then she leaned a hip against the counter.

"Bruce's anticipated maternity leave and Marques' EP has opened a lot of doors for me. They've asked me to oversee the launch with hopes of promoting me to A&R."

"Congrats!"

"Thanks, but hold it for now. I still need to get through this project."

"So, basically it's an interview."

"Exactly."

"How can I help?" Brione dropped her head and chuckled at the faint sounds of Eliana's clapping. Eliana could make it happen without her, but Brione wanted to see her friend succeed. "I didn't say yes yet."

"But you will." Eliana blew a kiss through the phone. "I want to host a release party in Houston, and I'd love to bring you in. It pays good, and I'm almost certain I can get you the gig."

"Really? But I've never done a music event."

"Don't worry about that. Your work is impeccable, you're organized, timely, and you work well under extreme pressure. Are you free Saturday?"

"Yes, how about ten?"

"That's perfect. Get together your portfolio and let's

meet at the cafe on Saturday. I'll try to get either Bruce or Marques there too. That way I can cross two tasks off my list at once."

"I like the sound of that."

"You would, Miss Planner Chic. I maintain, where you thrive. One day, I'll grow up to be just like you."

Brione shook her head as if Eliana could see her. "No, ma'am. Grow up to be like you, and you'll be just fine."

"The thought of peanut butter and honey back in business is enticing don't you think."

"Houston ain't ready for us," Brione added.

Eliana's robust laughter rang through the phone. "Girl, if only they knew! And for totally selfish reasons, it would be a lifesaver to have your help *and* get to spend time with you without you skipping out on me."

They haven't seen each other in years, for one reason or another. But Brione missed her too. "I got you. When we're done, they're going to beg you to take that position. And I'll be there at 9:45 ready to rock n' roll."

"Awesome. I'll text you if anything changes. I gotta go, we're about to land." Eliana said.

"Be safe." The microwave beeped.

"I will. Love you Peanut Butter." Eliana giggled.

"Love you too Honey." They disconnected, Brione stood staring at the phone for a minute considering their long friendship.

Eliana was her roommate in college, their running

nicknames came when all they could afford was Ramen noodles, and peanut butter and jelly, except Eliana, liked hers with honey or syrup.

Music was Eliana's passion like organizing events was Brione's. However, she knew her love of centerpieces and tulle could not lead to her desired destination.

Brione gathered her hot food from the microwave and walked to the dining room, she turned into an office. She stared at the stack of textbooks. She entered law school for two reasons: money and time. The family connections between the Bradleys and her parents guaranteed her seat. But her high GPA landed her a full ride.

She cleared a space for her bowl, tonight she'd study and tomorrow she'd order pizza and work on her portfolio. She lowered into the chair in front of her laptop, placing her food aside. She opened the oversized law book and turned to the cases she needed to read and analyze for class tomorrow.

She leaned over the keyboard and forked a chunk of lasagna, she cradled her hand beneath it to keep the sauce from dripping onto her expensive textbooks. She popped it into her mouth and did a chair dance as the ricotta cheese and Italian sausage made her taste buds happy, momentarily overlooking that it almost burnt her tongue. She pushed the bowl back to let it cool and read the first legal case when her phone rang again.

The little face on the screen made her heart race with joy.

"Hello, Sweet Pea." Her voice trembled, she took a deep breath.

"Hi!" Brione could envision her chubby cheeks, full eye lashes, and radiant smile.

"I think this is the best surprise I've had all day." Her giggle warmed Brione's heart. "How was school today?"

Kayla talked about crayons and finger painting. Her new best friend and a boy pulling her pigtails. All the things Brione had to experience by phone and not in person. And as soon as the call started it ended, sending exaggerated kisses through the phone to the tune of Kayla's sweet laughter with promises of talking with her again on Saturday.

Life wasn't fair. That was too tall of an order.

Brione used the fork to cut into the cooler lasagna. She had stopped crying about it and questioning why long ago, instead she dealt with it, taking blow by blow and somehow managing to bounce back. But tonight she wanted to sit in it. From the sting of the scheduled phone calls to Stewart consistently dangling their freedom like cheese enticing a rat, reminding herself that she had a plan. This ache in her chest was only temporary.

One day she and Kayla would live under the same roof. Holding on to this goal kept her in one piece.

Kayla motivated Brione to work hard and she vowed not to repeat the same mistake twice. Men like the dreamy caramel sex god Eliana drooled over were bad news. Stewart was one of them. He walked into a room and every woman—married, single, it didn't matter—wanted him. She'd thought herself lucky.

Brione snickered at her foolish youth. None of them cared about what she wanted in life. Her goals. Her desires. To the Bradleys, her parents, Stewart, she was their pawn, their minion, their tool. *So they thought.*

She couldn't afford to crack. She ate the rest of her dinner, deciding to study first then get her portfolio together for her meeting with Eliana.

To get Kayla back, she needed money and landing the job with Eliana to organize Marques' event could be the break she'd prayed for.

*W*alking into Coffee Confessions had a ring of a homecoming for Marques Carter. He had spent many days hanging around waiting on Bruce to finish a shift before they went to the studio. Houston saved him and got his life back on course. Now that he was back, he hoped lightning would strike again for them.

He pulled the baseball cap lower to disguise himself. The release of his first official video last week gave him more than his usual double takes. In Atlanta, he couldn't go anywhere without people recognizing him, here offered a reprieve. But he didn't want to take any chances, welcoming the way people bumped right past him. It added another reason he loved being back in Houston.

Marques arrived early to meet with Bruce. He scanned the room, spotting a few empty tables and made his way to the line. He lifted his head to read the menu when he felt a soft bump behind him. He turned around and had to glance down at a petite woman.

"Excuse me." She held up a hand then reached out to stabilize a mug rocking back and forth on the shelf. "I was trying to miss the stroller and then the display and…" Her voice stalled as she finally looked up at him. Her lips parted in surprise. "Huh, sorry."

He chuckled. "I think I'll live."

She nodded without speaking as their gazes held. Marques let his eyes survey her light brown skin paired with jet black hair. It was curled softly brushing the sides of her face in a chic bob. Her heart-shaped face and doe eyes held curiosity as her full lashes brushed her high cheekbones with each exaggerated blink behind black frames. But when he zeroed in on her full lips coated with a hint of gloss, her tongue darted out and a groan reached his ears. He didn't know if it came from him or her.

"Andrew Carter." Using his legal name seemed appropriate as he extended a hand ready to see if her skin was as soft as it appeared.

"Brione Allen." Her smooth husky tone reminded him of a midnight radio jockey. The type of voice that held intrigue, mystery, and allure.

She accepted his hand and lightning passed from her touch through his body. *Damn.* Her eyes flashed to meet his as his heart rate tripled. He studied her thoughtfully, appreciating the heat lingering in the depths of her brown eyes.

"Welcome to Coffee Confessions, give in to your guilty pleasure. How can I be of service?" The barista behind the counter asked and Marques was at a loss for words. He still held her delicate hand in his thinking Miss Brione Allen was a guilty pleasure he'd gladly give in to. But judging by the penetrating stare she gave him as she snatched her hand away from his, he doubted she was on the menu.

"I'm sorry, I need a moment to review the menu. Brione after you." He extended his hand towards the counter and she stepped forward. She appeared as surprised as he was. The chemistry between them was as real as the nose on his face.

"Huh, sure." She stepped to the counter and tossed her purse on her shoulder like a barrier between them. *No, baby girl, that purse ain't gonna save you.*

She started to order and the sounds of the room faded into oblivion as Marques scanned the length of her body, the curve of her backside, and…

"And for you sir?" The barista wiggled his eyebrows. Heat rose to Marques' face, *caught*. But her hips were too tempting to ignore in pants that left no curve to the imagination.

"Our order is not tog—"

"Make it two of what she's having." He passed his credit card and turned back to Brione.

"That's not necessary."

"You're welcome," he teased, her expression much too severe for him.

Her eyes softened, "Thank you."

Brione stepped to the side and waited as Marques collected his receipt. They stood in heated silence both snagging discreet glances at the other waiting for their coffee. He had no clue what she ordered, thankfully he wasn't allergic to anything.

His senses were ablaze with her nearness. The closest comparison would be the moment he completed a new song. It gave the dueling emotions of exhilaration and exhaustion simultaneously.

"Are you off to work today?" He noticed the button up blouse and dress slacks.

"No, I'm meeting a friend. And you?"

"Business." She scanned his body in a sweeping motion. He wore a baseball cap with jeans and shirt. His goal was to blend in with the good people of Houston. He wished now that he'd given it more thought. Her mouth took on an unpleasant twist. "What you don't approve of my casual attire?"

"Oh no. I think it must be nice."

He searched her eyes and wished he could read her mind. The barista called his name for the order. Marques passed a cup to her and grabbed his own. The place was filling up quickly. He snagged a table and pulled out a chair for her.

"Join me while you wait." She hesitated. "Please." Brione slowly lowered to the chair. The floral scent of her perfume couldn't compete with the aroma of the coffee beans but it was a soft statement of her presence in the busy cafe.

Marques sat across from her finding it hard to contain the odd sensation in the pit of his stomach. He took a drink of the hot coffee to distract himself. The taste of caramel and whipped cream warmed his mouth. "This is delicious. What is it?"

"A custom drink. It's my favorite." She lifted the cup to her mouth and took a sip too. Remnants of her gloss left on the white lid.

"I'll have to get this again." He grabbed his phone and snapped a picture of the sleeve. "So Brione tell me, are you from Houston?"

She sat her cup on the table, pulling closer. Their knees brushed, her eyes widened. "No."

He waited for her to continue, she crossed her hands over the table. "Are you always this talkative?"

Her husky laughter rippled through the air. "No, it takes me a minute to warm up to people."

He nodded. Brione dropped her hands to her lap, "What about you? Are you from here?"

"No, I'm from Georgia."

"You said you're here on business. What type of business are you in?"

"I'm in a family business. I'm taking a little time off before we enter a busy season." It was obvious she didn't recognize him. It made him relax, he didn't feel "on."

"Do you travel often?" She asked.

"Not as often as I'd like."

"So you enjoy traveling?"

He nodded, "I do. It is a love of mine, I acquired it as a child. I traveled a lot with my parents." He took a drink of his coffee. He joined his father on many tours over the years. "The food, architecture, music, museums, I love all of it."

"Where all have you visited?" The warmth of her smile echoed in her voice.

He crossed his arms over his chest and extended his legs. "I visited, at last count, 40 or so of the great states of America. I've hit the tourist spots. Australia, Canada, South Africa, Rome, London, Egypt, I love it there too. Dubai, New Zealand, India, China, Morocco, Italy, Bali. There are more but you put me on the spot."

"Tell me about your favorite place." She leaned over the table and rested her chin in her hand. Her eyes bright and inquisitive.

"Uh..." her smile made it hard to think straight, he searched his mind, "I can't pick just one. My most recent trip was to Bora Bora."

"That place is on my wish list." A smile danced on her lips, heat coursed through his veins. *Get a grip!*

"Put a star by it. It is a place you'll never forget. The warmth of the water. Its vibrant turquoise color. There's something magical and healing about the island."

Her expression stilled and grew serious.

"Add this one to your wish list too." He wanted to see her smile again. "Torres del Paine National Park."

The spark returned. "Where is that?"

Marques leaned forward enjoying the light in her eyes. "It's in Chile. There's more sheep than people but the valleys are the most vibrant green and the sky the bluest blue you'll ever see. There is a small window when the weather is appropriate but it is worth it." He winked and something told him she mentally noted every word.

He wondered what she was thinking as she dropped her head, brushing her hair behind her ears. Her phone buzzed against the table and Brione glanced down at the screen.

"That's my friend." She held up her phone and finished her coffee. "We have to reschedule."

She stood from the table and leaned over to toss the empty cup in the trash.

"Would you like another?"

"No, I have studying to do."

"Studying?" He hoped to prolong her departure.

"I'm a law student." The glimmer in her eyes dulled.

"If I remember correctly there are three of them here."

"You are absolutely correct." She placed her purse on her shoulder and picked up a black portfolio. He missed that earlier.

"Would you like to grab lunch or something?"

"I really need to go." She shook her head and

glanced at her phone. "Thank you for the coffee and the conversation." An easy smiled played at the corners of her mouth.

"No, thank you for this wonderful concoction." He held up the cup shaking it.

"You're welcome. Have a nice day." She turned to leave and he reached for her arm.

"Take my number. I'm in town for a couple weeks. I *really* would like to see you again."

"I don't have time. I—"

"Take it...just in case. Pass me your phone and I'll enter it."

She searched his eyes for so long he thought she'd say no again.

"Okay." She hesitantly passed her unlocked phone, holding the top with the tip of her fingers, as if trying to avoid his touch.

He entered his personal cellphone number and placed the phone in her open palm. "I'll talk with you soon."

CHAPTER 3

*B*rione sat to study for finals, she had two weeks left before summer break. But his voice, his smile barraged her. "Study Bri!"

Thoughts of coffee with Andrew had her head in the clouds. The way his head fell back when he laughed. The twinkle in his eyes when he teased her. It was a chasm in time that passed too fast, she wanted more.

Closing her eyes she estimated his height was close to six feet, the outlines of his shoulders strained against the fabric of his shirt. He stood before her with his hands shoved in his pockets and a killer smile wide with perfect white teeth. His classically handsome features made him beautiful for a man.

People passed their table slowing to gawk at him, not once did he look away or acknowledge their presence. She wondered what his hair looked like beneath the cap but figured it really didn't matter. The man could be bald and she was sure she'd find him absolutely breathtaking—star quality.

Brione shook her head trying to rattle the images of him from her memories. But it proved impossible.

She tried reading the case at least ten times with no luck. But his soft encouragement, add this one to your wish list, rendered it impossible. Adding him to her list sound better. *Forget it.*

She opened her laptop and clicked on an internet browser. She typed in, Torres del Paine National Park and pressed enter. The results populated, her inner child didn't know where to start. She squealed stomping her feet beneath the table to release the energy. Pictures, she'd start there.

Brione clicked on "Images." The pictures before her eyes made her lean into the monitor. There were mountains, valleys, glaciers, snow, a winter heaven. What had he done during his visit? Did he hike? Was he alone? Was it as cold as it appeared?

She grabbed her phone and went back to his contact. And she noticed the note, Call me and let's have dinner sometime. She had stared at it for most of her *non-effective* study time.

She could send a text.

Her fingers hovered over the screen. No. She shook her head, and then what? He'd text her back and want to talk on the phone. She put the phone back on the table. Music. That would help.

She stood and turned on the wireless speaker, stopping by the kitchen for some water. Back at the coffee table, she sat in front of her textbook. She untwisted the top off the plastic bottle and took a cool drink. She scanned her phone for some music, pressed play and turned back to the case.

Brione read through several immigration cases for class. Her doorbell rang and she glanced at the clock. She wasn't expecting anyone, she never had guests except... She stood up and walked to the door and glanced through the peephole. Her heart dropped to her feet. *What is he doing here?*

Stewart leaned into the doorbell. *Ding dong. Ding dong. Ding dong.*

"I know you're there. Open up and stop staring at me through the peephole."

Brione jerked back, placing her back against the door. She cracked her knuckles and exhaled a shaky breath. Her palms sweaty, she looked down at her t-shirt and leggings. Her clothes didn't matter. But she felt more in control in a suit. Less like the young woman that fell for his smile and honey-laced words only to get stung by a wasp.

"You can do this Bri," she whispered running her wet hands down her pants. She clutched one hand in the other to still her shaking limbs. "This is your space. You are in control."

Ding dong. Ding dong. Ding dong.

"I'm not leaving." He stated.

She placed a hand on the handle and unlocked the bolt. She peeked through the opening created by the chain. "What do you want?"

"I promise this is not the way you want to handle this situation." He leveled his deadly stare.

"I'm studying."

"I guess Kayla will call you next week then. Give you time to study." He stepped back never breaking eye contact with her. She unlatched the chain, stepping back as he strolled in like he owned the place.

Brione closed the door. Stewart was like the boogeyman. People refute its existence until it pops up under your bed.

He sat on the couch and leaned back. "Are you always this rude to your guests?" He stretched his arms across the cushions, obviously comfortable. "Can I get some water, sweet tea, a sandwich? Damn." He laughed at his own joke.

"You didn't drive to Houston for water or a sandwich. So stop with the dramatics. What do you want?"

"What I've always wanted, *you.*"

Stewart Bradley knew how to pop up on her doorstep when she felt confident, when she finally decided to not let him push her around, then he emerged from the shadows to call her bluff.

"Have a seat? I won't bite."

The invisible shackles clanked around her ankles as she sat in the chair closest to the door. "What do you want Stewart?"

"How are you?" His eyes scanned her body. She wrapped her arms protectively around her waist.

"I'm fine."

"When did you cut your hair and what's up with your clothes?"

"Stewart I'm studying." His mother was always dressed to perfection including a string of white pearls. He wanted a clone of Mrs. Bradley, the thought of her old sweats and short hair irking him brought a smile to her face. "And I like my bob."

"Is this how you're carrying yourself nowadays?"

"Is that why you visited? If so, we can end this conversation here and now." She swallowed hard.

"Don't let law school go to your head. This is still my show."

"Why don't you move on and let us move on too?

"There is no *us* without me," he growled. "You got into law school because of me. You can't care for Kayla without a job. What about her education? Her tutors? Her nanny? And don't forget about your pops." His glare intimidating. "I will deliver his career in a wastebasket. Is that what you want? Do you want to ruin everyone's lives because of your selfishness?"

The boogeyman live and in living color. Panic was

rioting inside her gnawing away at her confidence. Gnawing away at her plans and dousing her hope.

She once trusted this man and thought he loved her. That was the face of love. It was laughable. Her tongue felt thick and her nerves made it hard to form a coherent thought. She was tired of him pushing her around.

Don't let him push you around. Brione couldn't trust that voice, hadn't she invited him into her life in the first place. She dropped her head, stirring uneasily in the chair, hoping to hide the shame from his probing eyes. It was the cost of trusting an untrustworthy person. A person who valued self-ambition and greed over people. *How had I missed it?*

"Are you done playing with me?" His nostrils flared with fury.

She nodded, fear splintered her heart.

"Good." The storm clouds left his eyes. "Mom wants us to set a date."

She squeezed her eyes shut gripping the arms of the chair. "Stewart you don't want to marry me. We have nothing in common—"

"Nothing in common? We have *everything* in common. Let me shoot it to you straight. I want a date or so help me, Brione Allen, I'll bury you and your father's dreams of sitting in the Oval Office. And I'll ensure you never ever see our daughter again." He ground the words out through clenched teeth. "Understand?"

"Yes."

Continue Reading...

**Get Your Copy on Amazon
or Read in Kindle Unlimited!**

Blazin' Love (Contemporary Romance)

Platinum Love (Book 1)

Privileged Love (Book 2)

Exclusive Love (Book 3)

Chosen Love (Book 4)

Special Love (Book 5)

Absolute Love (Book 6)

Pretend for Me (A Short Story)

Devoted Love (Book 7)

Select Love (Book 8)

Lavish Love (Book 9)

Total Love (Book 10)

Conspiracy Ink Series (Romantic Suspense)

Veiled Conspiracy (re-release Summer 2019)

Forbidden Chords Series (Contemporary Romance)

Rockstar Secrets (Book 1)

Rockstar Sinners (Book 2)

Rockstar Savages (Book 3)

Waiting for You (A Short Story)

This Song's for You (A Short Story)

Precious Stones Series (Romantic Suspense)

Before Black Diamond (Prequel)

Black Diamond (Book 1)

African Emerald (Book 2)

Fire Opal (Book 3)

Ready for Love Series (Sweet Romance)

Caramel Surprise (Book 1)

Love's Hope (Book 2)

Hidden Desire (Book 3)

Ready for Love Boxed Set (Books 1 - 3)

Smith Pact Duo (Contemporary Romance)

Yuki's Luck (Book 1)

Tempting Asher (Book 2)

Smith Surprise (Book 3)

When It Comes to Love Boxed Set (Books 1 - 3)

See all of my books on my website:

http://www.janesedixon.com/books.

ABOUT THE AUTHOR

Ja'Nese Dixon pens tales of romance in several sub-genres. But her favorites are the ones that manage to keep readers sitting on the edge of their seats lying to themselves about reading "just one more chapter".

Ja'Nese is an avid reader and coffee drinker, who also loves to run, cook, and craft. Her ultimate goal as a writer is to give you a little "staycation" with every story. And she aims to make this present story no exception. Sit back, grab a snack and enjoy.

Ja'Nese calls Houston home with her husband, three kiddos and a four-legged diva dog.

Visit her website at www.janesedixon.com if you enjoy romance, suspense and good stories.

Subscribe to Ja'Nese Newsletter "Reader's Staycation" for reader exclusives, regular giveaways and more.

Stay in Touch:
www.janesedixon.com
info@janesedixon.com

facebook.com/AuthorJaNeseDixon

twitter.com/janesedixon

instagram.com/authorjanesedixon

amazon.com/author/janesedixon

bookbub.com/authors/ja-nese-dixon

ABOUT THE PUBLISHER

Purpose Prevails Publishing
2231B Center St. STE 144
Deer Park, TX 77536
www.purposeprevailspublishing.com